THE PORTRAIT

THE PORTRAIT

•

Hazel Statham

AVALON BOOKS
NEW YORK

Published by Avalon Books, an imprint
Thomas Bouregy & Co., Inc.
160 Madison Avenue, New York, NY 10016

Library of Congress Cataloging-in-Publication Data

Statham, Hazel.
   The portrait / Hazel Statham.
         p.   cm.
   ISBN 978-0-8034-7787-2
   1. Aristocracy (Social class)—England—19th century—
Fiction.   2. Great Britian—History—19th century—Fiction.
I. Title.
   PS3619.T3823P67 2010
   813' .6—dc22

                                                    2010016293

PRINTED IN THE UNITED STATES OF AMERICA
ON ACID-FREE PAPER
BY HADDON CRAFTSMEN, BLOOMSBURG, PENNSYLVANIA

To the light of my life,
my beautiful grandson, Daniel

Prologue

The Battle of Salamanca, Spain, July 22, 1812

The French were in disarray and taking refuge in retreat when a brief bombardment of cannon fire issued from their ranks. Amid the onslaught, Marchant's Cavalry made good their escape, but an explosion sent Edward Thurston, the new twenty-seven-year-old Earl of Sinclair, reeling from his saddle.

In just one brief moment the tall, athletic earl, who had led his men so enthusiastically in the attack, lay near death, his life's blood seeping into the muddy ground. Briefly his gray eyes registered pain before closing in blessed oblivion.

Seeing an injured, riderless horse racing at his side, one of the young English officers, Major Anthony Drake, sharply drew rein, fiercely swinging his horse around.

"My God, Ned!" he cried, heedlessly urging his horse once more toward the cannon fire and throwing himself to the ground beside the inert figure of his friend.

"My God! My God!" was all he could cry as panic and bile rose at sight of the devastation wrought on his friend's noble frame by the blast.

Another rider, a sergeant, appeared at his side and threw himself from his saddle. "We must get him onto my horse, sir," he said urgently. "Help me lift him." And between them, despite the bombardment, they raised the lifeless form from the mud.

Amid heavy rifle fire, they flung Sinclair over the horse's withers before vaulting into their saddles and furiously galloping back to their own lines.

The air inside the field medical tent was oppressive. The wounded and dying lay on pallets, with scarcely enough room to walk between them. The battle had been won, but the cost in human suffering was high.

Dr. Pyke, the surgeon, stood beside the cot of the young nobleman, who lay with eyes closed against the sights around him. "The left arm must come off at the shoulder, sir," he said firmly.

Immediately Sinclair's eyes opened wide. "By God, it will not!" he replied fiercely from between bloodless lips thinned with pain. "I'll have none of your butchery!" The scarlet of the wounds to his left cheek and torso stood out in stark contrast to his ashen skin and the dark hair that clung to his fevered brow. His left arm hung from its ragged joint, a useless, bloody appendage.

Pyke spoke in measured tones, as if every vestige of strength had been drained from him during his attendance on the never-ending stream of casualties. "If the arm is not removed, I cannot guarantee the outcome, my lord."

Sinclair's eyes were bright with fever. "And you can if it's removed?" he sneered. "I think not!"

"No, sir, but we must at least try. I have been ordered—nay, commanded—to do all that I can."

"By whom?"

"By the great man himself."

"Then you can tell Wellington to go to blazes. I'll have no sawbones hacking at me."

The tent flap was pushed aside, and Wellington himself entered.

"My Lord . . ." began Pyke, but Wellington raised a hand.

"You need not tell me," he said. "I heard all. Ignore what Sinclair says. 'Tis the laudanum speaking. He knows not what he's saying. Remove the arm."

Chapter One

Hertfordshire, England, December 1, 1812

To Sinclair, the impressive prospect of Fly Hall had never seemed more welcoming. In the waning, early-evening light, his gaze roamed lovingly over the sprawling, half-timbered Tudor mansion set deep within a valley, noting its gentle air of noble neglect. The weeds that sprang from paving and the ivy that shaded the windowpanes proved almost too much for him, since he knew such would not have been allowed if the old earl, his father, was alive.

It was a bittersweet homecoming. The journey had left him unbelievably weary, but the mere sight of the house, seen from its parkland approach, gave him a peace of mind he had not experienced for some while. He wished nothing more than to be within its familiar, welcoming portals.

His wounds still plagued him, and at times he swore he could still feel the fingers of his left hand moving. Alas, he'd heard of like cases among his fellow wounded and knew this to be nothing more than the effects of the amputation, which would disappear with time. He'd been assured that the angry

4

scarring to his body, where the cannonball had torn his flesh, would fade. Even now, the slight paling of the scar across his left cheek gave evidence of this.

The eyes remained the same, bright and alive, only the humor once seen there having waned. Stubble sprang from his cheeks and chin, and his dark hair curled at the nape of his neck, proving his need of a barber's services. He'd lain abed in a convent on the Portuguese border, along with others wounded in the encounter, and such niceties as barbering had, by necessity, been overlooked.

As the coach rounded the final bend in the driveway and the house came fully into view, he reached into his greatcoat pocket and took out an elegantly framed miniature of a young lady with smiling eyes and dark curls.

"You see, my love, we finally arrive," he said in hushed tones before carefully replacing the miniature. He had carried it with him throughout the campaign, and it was only the sight of her face, during his delirium, that had prevented his senses from deserting him. In the convent, his reliance on the portrait had been noted, but wisely none had commented, so fiercely did he protect it.

The coach halted before the imposing front door, and even before the groom was able to let down the steps, the doors to the house were flung wide, and, all formality forgotten, two of the menservants ran forward.

Caring hands helped Sinclair to alight, supporting him into the familiar, half-paneled hallway, where a welcoming fire blazed in the large stone hearth. Immediately a chair was brought forward, into which he gratefully sank. His senses, long bereft of the familiar sights and sounds of the house, drank in its comforting warmth, and a sense of peace settled over him. Even the dark wainscoting, which he had once thought outmoded, appeared to welcome him, and his eyes closed briefly with the relief of being home.

Croft, an elderly retainer who appeared almost as ancient as the house itself, hurried forward, his weathered countenance full of concern. "Your chamber has been made ready. We will assist you there when you are rested, my lord," he informed his master, bowing with obvious difficulty.

" 'My lord'?" Sinclair queried, raising a quizzical eyebrow. "You were never usually so formal."

"Aye, but you were not master then," Croft replied with a dry chuckle. "I can't call you Mister Edward now that the old earl has gone. It would not be seemly."

Sinclair offered a weary smile. "And when have you cared for 'seemly'? I will not believe myself home if I'm to be treated with such unfamiliar reverence."

Rose, a small plump woman who acted as both housekeeper and cook and appeared as ancient as her husband, Croft, issued from below stairs wiping her hands on her apron. "Mister Edward!" she cried, her pleasant countenance wreathed in smiles. "There's pheasant soup, pork with apple, and chicken-and-ham pie—everything you like. We shall have you to rights in no time."

Heartened by her enthusiastic welcome, the earl's smile widened into a grin, and he straightened slightly in the chair. "There, that's a welcome worth coming home for. Though I may not be able to do justice to your cooking at this precise moment, Rose, it is something I have sorely missed. Believe me when I say that even the finest cooks in the military can't hold a candle to your excellent table."

Rose flushed with pleasure and, standing with arms akimbo, rounded on the other servants, her voice gruff with emotion. "What are you all standing there for, you great ninnies? Take the master to his room. He must be tired after his journey. Once he is made comfortable, we can see what is needed." Then, turning to the earl, she said, "Dr. Wilmot said that we were to inform him of your arrival, sir, and he would come at once to attend to you."

Sinclair sighed heavily, his smile disappearing, replaced by a look of tired resignation. "Then I pray you will allow me a little time to recover from my journey before you send word to him. I have been poked and prodded enough over these past weeks; one more day without his ministrations will make no difference. I shall retire."

The ivy, teased by the morning breeze, scratched at Sinclair's bedroom window, reminding him that he was indeed returned to his beloved Fly. Dr. Wilmot arrived shortly after nine, going immediately to his patient's bedchamber, eager to begin the examination of his childhood friend.

Lying on his large canopied bed, Sinclair bore his friend's professional examination with a stoicism born of necessity. He had learned by experience that he must endure what could not be avoided, and he waited until Wilmot completed his assessment before speaking.

As the doctor straightened from his examination, Sinclair said with deceptive lightness, "Come now, John, what's your opinion of me? Don't stand on ceremony. I have known you too long for there to be any reserve between us."

Wilmot smiled. "Your wounds are healing well enough, Edward, and although it will take some while, I do believe you will return to full strength."

Sinclair's voice dropped. "And what of the night terrors? Will they cease?"

"Almost certainly. They are the result of the amputation and the trauma to your body, but with time they will diminish."

"Time I don't have," the earl replied curtly, his gaze becoming distracted and his hand moving restlessly on the blue brocade quilt that Wilmot had placed back over him at the end of his examination. "Ironic, is it not? To the outside world 'twould appear that I have time aplenty, but you see, I have not. I am to be married, John. Or, more rightly, I *was* to be married. Yet how can I expect a wife to commit herself to the wreck I have become?"

"You are no wreck," the medic assured him. "It will take more than the loss of your arm to bring you low. Your strength will assuredly return."

Sinclair grimaced ruefully. "Ah, but my strength will not return my arm to me or make my form more pleasing to Lady

Jennifer, my betrothed. I'll carry these scars with me through life."

Wilmot saw the earl's agitation. "Your scars were gained honorably, Edward, and when you feel more yourself, you'll become reconciled to them."

Sinclair shook his head impatiently. "Tell that to a new bride. She will soon tire of such a husband. She will be repulsed by me, and who should blame her? Certainly not I."

"Women are such unpredictable creatures. It is oft noted that they can become devoted to the most unlikely of spouses, and if she loves you . . ."

"There you have the truth of it; I don't believe that she does. The betrothal was hastened because, like every other young buck of my generation, despite my father's protestations against his heir's laying himself open to such dangers, I was eager to hasten to war. Lady Jennifer and I knew each other for such a short time, with little opportunity to be private. In short, I must admit to its being a contrived marriage, a *mariage de convenance* brought about by our respective sires. I took my commission and hastened to Spain, as eager as any Englishman to face Old Boney. I have been too long away; we will be but strangers."

"Was there no communication between you?"

"We wrote very little, and I felt no desire to impart the horrors of war. I would shield her from such abominations. I preferred to keep my own counsel and instead encouraged her to tell me of the season's gaieties and divert my thoughts."

Wilmot appeared incredulous. "You made no effort to engage her affections?"

"How could I, from such a distance?"

"I would not have thought that to pose a problem to you, Edward. I always thought you a man of considerable address."

"If that be the case, how, then, am I to present her with who I have become? She's not even aware of the extent of my injuries, and I would wish to be the man she thought me when we became betrothed."

Wilmot raised his eyebrows in disbelief. "You've not informed her of the nature of your wounds?"

"I felt not the need to distress her with the details."

The medic shook his head. "You take this desire to shield her too far, Edward. Surely it would have been wiser to have prepared her for your homecoming . . . ?"

Sinclair, his face set, raised a hand to silence the doctor. "My mind is made up. I shall release her from her promise. I wouldn't wish that she take me out of pity."

"There is no reason, once your wounds are thoroughly healed, you can't lead a full and healthy life," Wilmot replied, closing his bag with a snap and taking up his cloak. "The amputation has left you feeling low. You will feel completely different in a few months' time."

"But I don't have a few months, John. My betrothed has sent word that she is to visit me within the week, and then we shall see what strangers we have become. I have no illusions. She was but seventeen when the arrangements were made, and I have been away for over two years. She is still so young. The engagement was made at the instigation of her family; my prospects appealed to them. Now that I have ascended to the title, I will not be married for my rank and fortune, which is where my only desirability lies. Despite my disabilities, I would prefer to remain unwed than accept such a compromise."

"You are thoroughly convinced that the marriage should not go ahead? I can say nothing to persuade you otherwise?"

"Nothing can dissuade me."

"Then far be it from me to attempt to change your mind. You will no doubt take your own course."

"You may not have persuaded me, my friend, but in openly expounding it, I have convinced myself that the marriage should not take place and in so doing have shaken a burden from my shoulders."

"Then my visit has at least been of some use to you?"

"Undoubtedly!"

"You are now resolved to the issue?"

"Perfectly!"

"Then, my old friend, the only way is forward!"

On the morning of the promised visit from Lady Jennifer, Edward, having spent a restless night thinking of his betrothed, watched as rivulets of rain ran slowly down his bedchamber window. They singularly suited his mood. At dawn's first light he had raised himself up on his pillows, his thoughts filled with the pending reunion. Only now would he allow himself to dwell on thoughts of what might have been had he been returning to her as a whole man—a return he had anticipated so often during his time at war.

When Croft entered the room, the man was clearly surprised to find his master fully awake, his features drawn. "Have you not slept well, sir?" he asked, full of concern. "Shall I arrange for breakfast to be served here? Perhaps you should delay your foray to the lower floor until you are stronger."

"I will not receive Lady Jennifer in my bedchamber," Sinclair stated, pushing aside the coverlet and placing his feet on the floor. "I have two perfectly sound legs, and, with your aid in dressing, I'll entertain my visitor in the morning room. It has a pleasant and open aspect, and I wish not to appear dull for her visit."

Croft nodded and busied himself about the room. "The Holland covers have been removed from all the rooms, sir, and everything is as it should be. My Rose has seen to that. She has made ready your regimentals. . . ."

The earl pushed himself erect. "Then she need not have bothered. I'm not in the military now. I am a civilian and have no wish to cling to my uniform. Lay out the blue superfine— it will suffice."

"Aye, sir, I thought you might say that." Croft grinned and brought forward a chair for Sinclair. "Until your valet arrives from London and takes over its care, Rose has had your entire wardrobe refreshed."

Sinclair sat on the chair, not wishing to admit to the weakness he felt from rising, determined to greet his betrothed with at least some of his old vigor. "When my visitor arrives, serve refreshments immediately, and then I wish for no interruptions for the remainder of her visit. Is that quite clear?"

"Perfectly, sir."

"Then bring my razor, and help me prepare."

Once his dressing had been completed and Croft had been dismissed, the earl stood before the large mirror and examined the results. While not thoroughly pleased with what he saw, he felt some satisfaction at returning at last to his civilian clothing. The empty sleeve had been pinned to the breast of his coat, which, though still fitting the broad expanse of his shoulders, hung on his battle-hardened frame. He stood for a moment longer and made a mental note that a visit from his tailor should be arranged as soon as possible. Turning abruptly away from his reflection, he crossed to the dresser and, opening one of the drawers, took out the miniature.

He held it before him, a slow smile spreading over his countenance. Then, as if taken by a sudden decision, he crossed to the hearth and threw it into the newly lit fire. However, seeing the flames rise up to lick the edges of the frame brought a pain to his breast he could not bear, and, snatching up a pair of tongs, he bent quickly and retrieved it once more, unable to endure its destruction.

"Not yet. Not yet," he whispered to the sweet face that looked back at him. "It is too soon. I will have you with me a while longer. I cannot bear your going." Taking it once more to the dresser, he pulled out a fine linen handkerchief and, spreading it wide, laid the portrait within its folds and returned it to the drawer.

His shoulder and the wounds to his side ached. The long journey back to England had taken its toll on his resources, but, wishing not to evoke pity, he was determined to present no feeble form to his betrothed when she arrived. Instead, he pulled back his shoulders and, casting a final glance at the mirror, left his apartment and made his way to the breakfast room on the ground floor.

It was the first time he had ventured from his chamber since his arrival, and he felt the warmth of familiar surroundings once more envelop him, the only sadness being that his father was no longer present. It had been just before the battle at Albuera that he had heard of his death. However, the urgency of the situation in Spain had precluded his return, even though his desire was to be with his younger brother, Peregrine, whom he now found to be his ward. The boy, then but fifteen years of age, had gone to live with their married sister, Lady Flora Carlton, in Essex but was now in his first term at Oxford. Notice of the earl's return had been sent to Peregrine, and arrangements were in progress that he should return to Fly Hall at the end of term in two weeks' time. Edward had thought it prudent that his brother not return before the given date, as he wished to be more recovered from his journey for their reunion. Peregrine idolized him, and he wished to appear still strong.

Sinclair eased himself into the chair held for him at the breakfast table but, ignoring the collation Rose had deemed necessary to prepare, ordered the butler to bring him nothing but eggs and toast. He had no appetite, but it would appear churlish should he refuse all Rose's efforts on his behalf. However, while he drank a steaming cup of coffee, he merely toyed with the meal before finally pushing away his plate, which the butler immediately removed.

Lady Jennifer Lynton, a petite brunet, pushed aside her morning repast and rose hastily from the table.

"I have already told you, Arthur, I am determined to release the Earl of Sinclair from the engagement," she vowed, standing resolutely before her elder brother, her usually expressive blue eyes and sweet countenance holding a determination rarely seen.

Throwing aside his napkin and pushing his chair from the table, the Earl of Hawley said with equal asperity, "That you will not, my girl. It is all arranged, and no matter the circumstances, the marriage will go ahead."

"Don't you care that I have no desire whatsoever to be married?" she accused. "It was only to please Father that I agreed to it in the first place, and now that he's no longer with us, I feel no need to go through with it."

"More likely, now that you've met young Rothwell, you feel no need to go through with it. Ah, yes, I've seen you making calf's eyes at him, miss."

"That you have not," she cried, stamping her foot emphatically. "I have never made calf's eyes at anyone, let alone Lord Rothwell, whom I find insufferably self-centered and opinionated. It's just that . . . Well . . ."

"There, you can't give a good reason why you shouldn't become Sinclair's countess, can you?" declared Arthur with some aplomb. "Think of the benefits. He's well-bred with impeccable connections. He's also known to be extremely even-tempered, which must recommend him to any young bride."

"But, Arthur, I wish for more than an even temper from a husband. . . ."

"With your hoydenish ways, an even temper is a distinct advantage and much to be desired. How else would he be able to contend with your starts and fancies? No, I am determined that you will go through with the marriage."

"You want nothing more than to be free of me," Jennifer stated. "Frederick, too, for that matter. Indeed, if truth were told, you want the house to yourself so that you can marry Amelia Cheviot."

"And if I do, who can blame me? I will not play nursemaid to you and your brother. It wasn't my wish to be left guardian to my siblings. Surely you must realize just how repugnant the situation is to me."

"Frederick need not concern you—but you have made sure of that. He had no great desire to go up to Oxford, but you insisted. For myself, I have no more wish to live with you than you have to have me here, but I will not be pushed into marriage just to suit your purpose."

"You ever were an ungrateful chit," Arthur fumed, rising and making for the door. "But I warn you, refuse Sinclair, and you will find me less than charitable. Then see how far your face and fortune will get you when you're obliged to accept the first man who comes along. You will be glad to, if only to remove yourself from my influence." With a flourish he was gone, leaving Jennifer to stare angrily after him.

However, once she was alone, her mood underwent a complete turnabout, and an air of uncertainty overtook her. With lagging steps she left the breakfast parlor to go to her own apartments to prepare for her visit. Nonetheless, upon entering her bedchamber, instead of calling for her maid to help her dress for her journey, she went to sit in the window seat. Resting her head in her cupped hand, she gazed blankly through the casement.

When she thought of the Earl of Sinclair, as she had done quite often since the event of their betrothal, it was with very mixed emotions. At first, when the betrothal had been announced, being the envy of all her contemporaries, she was filled with excitement, but the feeling had been short-lived. No sooner had the notice of the engagement been posted in the *Gazette* than her betrothed had found it necessary to dispatch himself to Spain, and he had seemed in no hurry to return. Even his letters had been very formal, hardly what one would expect from a would-be bridegroom, and she had found it difficult to respond to his impersonal tone.

Even when he had been wounded, he'd not found it necessary to communicate that fact to her. She had received news of it from George Reynolds, the brother of her friend Anne, and he had only heard of it by chance. She knew not the nature of the earl's wounds or their extent and felt piqued at what she perceived as the cavalier way in which she'd been treated. Did he think her of so little consequence that he'd denied her the knowledge of his injuries? Indeed, she had only learned of his impending return by way of a brief communication from Reynolds, who had gleaned the information from his position at Whitehall. She had immediately sent a note to Fly, determined to inform the earl of her decision at the earliest opportunity.

"I am thoroughly out of patience with you, Edward Thurston," she said to the empty room. "I will not be all but ignored for more than two years and then be expected to trot up the aisle with you. Indeed I will not!" She wouldn't admit to what extent saying those words only served to deepen the hurt she felt, but, rallying, she called for her maid and with some determination prepared for her visit.

Entering the hallway at Fly, Jennifer asked her cousin Eleanor, who acted as chaperone, to await her there. Despite the impropriety, she wished for no witness to the interview with her betrothed, desiring whatever words were spoken to remain private. It took much persuading, but eventually Eleanor, much against her better judgment, succumbed to her young relative's pleadings and allowed herself to be cozily seated by the large fireplace, glad of its welcoming warmth after the chill of the carriage.

Hearing the sounds of arrival, the earl rose from his chair in the morning room and prepared to meet his intended. Something in the region of his chest clenched at the thought of the impending interview, but he schooled his countenance to greet her with an equanimity he was far from feeling.

Almost immediately the door opened, and Croft announced Lady Jennifer. Full of resolve, her skirts swishing with the crispness of her steps, she came quickly into the light-filled, blue and gold salon. As the door closed quietly behind her, she came to an abrupt halt.

Finding it difficult to advance farther into the room, she visibly blanched at the extent of Sinclair's injuries, her expressive eyes widening at sight of his altered appearance. Nothing could have prepared her for the emotions the mere sight of him evoked, and whatever words she might have uttered died unsaid.

Ignoring his wildly leaping emotions at seeing her once more, Edward drank in the delicacy of her features and form and, gathering his cloak of resolve about him, quickly closed the gap between them. Taking her cold fingers in his warm clasp, he raised them dutifully to his lips, feeling them tremble in his hold. His eyes never left her face, and he realized that there was no guile about her as he watched the mix of emotions that chased across her pale countenance. In that instant he knew he had made the right decision to end the betrothal.

"My lord, I . . ." she began, but her voice failed, and he saw tears well up in her beautiful eyes.

"Will you not be seated, Lady Jennifer?" he said, leading her to a chair by the hearth. "Croft will bring refreshments, and after a cup of tea I am sure you will feel more the thing." Releasing her hand, he stood before her as she sank into the chair. He found it necessary to concentrate, to keep his voice neutral, so that she would not be aware of his inner turmoil. Grateful that he was at least allowed to retain his pride, he was relieved that he showed no signs of the physical weakness that had laid him so low.

"I realize my appearance must come as quite a shock to you," he said with an incongruous smile.

She half rose, but he held up his hand to forestall her, and she once more sank back against the cushions. All former irritation forgotten, she was unable to put into words what she was feeling at that precise moment and was relieved when a light tapping on the door heralded an interruption.

Croft came into the room with a tray full of a light repast, which he placed on a low table set at their side, whilst a butler brought in a tea tray and set it on a small table beside Jennifer.

Busying herself with pouring the tea, she set up a flow of inconsequential conversation in the hope of presenting a diversion. She never allowed her eyes to wander from her task, dreading the moment when she would be forced to acknowledge the situation. However, as she handed the cup to Sinclair, the words died on her lips as she became aware of his intense scrutiny.

Seeing her unease, Edward straightened himself in his chair, saying in a subdued tone, "Lady Jennifer, I think it only fair that I bring about a swift end to your disquiet. I see what effect my injuries have on you, and believe me when I say that I quite understand. I am not so insensitive as to not realize just how devastating it would be if you were forced to ally yourself to such an individual as I have become. I would not wish it on you."

She would have given an answer, but he slowly shook his head. "There is no need to attempt to put the matter delicately. I am quite sure you realize, as do I, that to continue with the engagement would be disastrous. Therefore, I will not equivocate on the issue. I release you from your promise. The wedding will not take place."

"It is not your wish that we should marry?" she asked, paling still further.

"It is not. I will send a retraction to the *Gazette* immediately. It will be understood that I have been too long away, and who should blame us if our sentiments have undergone a change during that time? Indeed, it will be seen that I am the cause of the rift, so you need not fear censure."

"Are my feelings on the matter not to be considered then, sir?" she demanded.

"I don't think you know what your feelings are at this precise moment," he replied, noting the indignant tilt of her chin and the militant look in her eye. "If you would but be guided by me, I'm sure you will see the right of it and will be relieved to be rid of me."

"I am beginning to think that I shall," she said, coming abruptly to her feet and nearly upsetting the tea tray in the process. "I'm excessively grateful to you for pointing it out to me. You have saved me the need to deliberate further on the matter."

He, too, came to his feet and bridged the distance between them to take her hand in his. "You may not think it now, but you will come to be grateful to me for making the decision," he said earnestly. "Let not your sentiments at this moment cloud your judgment. You see me as a case for pity, and that is not what I would wish. I will not allow you to take me when such emotions rule."

"You are quite right, sir," she snapped, withdrawing her hand from his warm clasp. "I would not wish you to think that I take you out of sympathy; therefore, I see the sense of it." She did not understand why his words piqued her so. Had it not been her own intent to end the betrothal?

An unfathomable look came into his eyes. "I hope we may still meet as friends."

"As friends? I see no reason why we should not," she replied coolly, deciding her reaction was that of resentment because it had been he who had uttered the words that ended the betrothal and not she.

Relieved, he smiled. "Then we are in agreement?"

"Most certainly. You have taken a burden from my mind. I, too, had wondered at the sense of continuing with the engagement and had reached the same decision as you. Now we are both free to continue with our lives unhindered."

"Have you felt the betrothal a hindrance?" he asked with some concern.

She colored with confusion. "Yes . . . no . . . I don't know what I have felt. We had become as strangers, and you were so far away. . . ." Her voice faltered, and she refused to meet his gaze.

"Then the decision to end it is the right one, and you may recommence your life without its burden. Now that the matter is settled, we can be easy in each other's company. Won't you be seated and take some tea with me? Talk to me for a while. I am in dire need of civilized conversation."

When the time came for Jennifer to leave Fly, Edward escorted his former betrothed and her companion to their chaise. Watching from the shallow steps that led to the gravel drive, he raised his hand in farewell as the equipage rolled down the long driveway, waiting until it disappeared from view before turning back to the hall.

Repairing immediately to his apartment, he went straight to

the dresser and pulled wide the drawer. Without taking it from its resting place, he opened up the handkerchief and looked once more at the delicate face in the portrait.

"The deed is done, my love. The deed is done," he said quietly, and, once more folding the cloth, he gently closed the drawer.

When the earl had retired to his bedchamber and Croft was closing Fly for the night, he became aware of a commotion on the driveway outside the front door. Drawing back the bolts, he stepped out into the frosty night air to see who would be arriving at such an unearthly hour. To his great surprise, the Honorable Peregrine Thurston was in the process of alighting from a hired coach. He was a young man of medium height, as fair as the earl was dark, yet still bearing a striking resemblance to his older brother. Following closely on his heels was another young man of about the same age and a large brown mastiff-like dog that lollopped up the steps and stood grinning at the retainer.

"What's all this, Master Perry?" demanded Croft, coming forward to greet the youngest member of the family. "Why aren't you at Oxford? We weren't expecting you for at least another week. Who is this you bring with you?"

Perry grinned good-naturedly. "Oh, take a powder, Croft. I—we've—been rusticated for the remainder of the term, so where else would we go but here?"

" 'Rusticated'?" repeated Croft, shaking his head and leading the way into the brightly-lit hall. "The master will not like that. He will not like that at all. Has he not enough to contend with, what with his injuries and such, without you finding it necessary to get yourself rusticated?"

Perry grinned. "Oh, Ned won't mind. He's a great gun and understands these things. He'll see how it was when I explain to him. He'll read me no lecture."

"I'm not so sure about that," said Croft, closing the large door and driving home the bolts in the aged wood. "It's not right that you should be causing him more trouble at a time like this."

"Is he very bad?" asked Perry, suddenly serious. "How is he, Croft? Is he in a great deal of pain? I can't bear it if he is."

"Whatever pain he's in, he bears very well. You will not hear him complain, and I do believe he is much improved from when he first arrived. He tires easily though, so you must not be wearing him out with your pranks."

"Told you he was made of stern stuff, Freddie," affirmed Perry, turning to his companion, a deceptively cherubic-looking young man of about his own height whose dark locks were in permanent wild disarray. "Go with Croft to the kitchen. I'm sure Rose will find you something. You will see that he's fed, won't you, Croft? We have had nothing to eat since breakfast, and then it was only the merest morsel. Had no money to buy food on the road, once the chaise had been paid for."

"Aye, I'll see he's fed, but you are not to go bothering the master at this time of night. He needs his rest. Leave it till morning."

"That I will not," replied Peregrine, starting toward the stairs, the large dog hard on his heels. "I will see him tonight, or I'll have no peace."

"You're not to take that great brute up to the master's room," remonstrated Croft. "He's in need of peace and quiet. Leave the dog here."

"Don't be such an old hen-worrier, Croft." Perry grinned. "Ned won't mind my waking him in the least, and I am sure he will be delighted to see Caesar. He's always been a good judge of dogs, and he will recognize the nobleness of his nature."

"Nobleness? Nobleness? When he stands drooling over his lordship's carpet? He's nothing but a big, dirty brute and will be seen for what he is. Your brother will soon send you away with a flea in your ear. You mark my words."

Taking no heed whatsoever of the retainer's words, Perry turned from the hall and ran up the stairs, taking them two at a time. Turning midway, he called Caesar to follow in his wake, and the large dog lumbered playfully after him, his large jowls emitting copious amounts of drool as he went.

Croft turned away, shaking his head as he went. For more than fifty years he'd served this noble family, and he had long since given up any hope of understanding the vagaries of youth. *Now, Master Ned, he had been a different kettle of fish,* he thought. *Even so, there had still been times when the old earl was obliged to read him a lecture and point out the error of his ways. Always very understanding, though, was Master Edward; he never held a grudge against his father.* Then Croft's grizzled countenance was transformed as, much to the surprise of the young gentleman he was now leading toward the kitchen, he let out a dry chuckle as he continued to silently reminisce. *There was that time when Master Edward was caught snatching apples in the orchard, and his sister, Miss Flora, took away the ladder. Such a noise he set up, shouting to be let down and threatening all manner of things he would do to the little miss. Almost two hours he was stuck up that tree until she relented and let him down. The old earl, not pleased, had thrashed Master Edward and banished the little miss to her room.*

Chapter Two

A lone candle set on the bedside table softly illuminated the earl's bedchamber, leaving the corners of the room deep in shadow.

"Rusticated?" expostulated Sinclair, raising himself on his pillows. He had not been asleep, merely dozing, but at the sound of his bedchamber door being so rudely opened had come fully awake to find his young brother standing at the foot of his bed.

"Only until next term," Perry hopefully assured him.

"And may I ask, in my ignorance, why, for no matter what length of time, you've been rusticated?"

"Well, you see, it was because of Caesar. . . ."

"And what, precisely, had the great Caesar to do with the matter?"

"Oh, not *the* great Caesar, Ned, just this one." Perry grinned engagingly as the huge dog raised himself up from the floor and laid his massive head on the bed, his doleful eyes examining its occupant.

The earl returned the stare, a slight twitching of his lips

threatening to betray his amusement, but he fought to keep the severity of his tone as he turned his regard to his brother. "You will no doubt appraise me, in your own good time of course, why this animal should be the cause of your suspension and how it came to be in your possession."

"Don't look so cross, Ned," said a penitent Peregrine. "They were going to use him for baiting, and I'm sure you can understand my need to rescue him."

"Undoubtedly. And how much did this 'rescue' cost you?"

"Ten guineas, sir."

"I didn't think you would own ten guineas this late into the term."

"I had only half that amount, but I borrowed the rest from Freddie. Freddie's a great pal, a real regular gun."

"So now I am obliged to bail you out to the tune of five guineas, am I?"

"If you would be so kind, I would be enormously grateful, Ned. I must tell you, though, that everything would've been fine if it hadn't been for that damned cat. . . ."

"Ah, now a cat comes into the narrative," replied the earl, as if enlightened.

"Well, I'm sure you will understand that even though it was the House Master's cat, Caesar felt *obliged* to give chase. No self-respecting dog would've been able to ignore such a challenge."

"May I ask why this perfectly understandable chase should have such dire results?"

"It was through the dining hall while we were at supper."

"Ah, that certainly does explain it," said the earl with a half smile, which he immediately attempted to hide. But it was too late. Peregrine, ever watchful of his brother's face, had seen its birth.

"Knew you would appreciate it, Ned." He grinned, his boyish countenance flushed. "Lord, if you could've seen the upset he caused. There was rice pudding for supper. . . ."

The earl laughed openly. "Then we must ensure not to consume the likes in his presence."

"Then he can stay?"

"After causing so much trouble, I suppose he must, if only to bear witness to your stupidity."

"You are the best brother a chap could have, Ned. Knew you could be relied on to understand."

"You will think me less than good when I tell you that your studies are to be continued despite your rustication. You will read the classics to me to improve your Latin."

Perry hung his head. "There's just one more thing I need explain, Ned. Freddie Lynton is with me."

"Don't tell me they rusticated him too?"

"Devil a bit, though I did warn him not to champion me. Now he daren't go home. Says there would be hell to pay. His brother is not as understanding of a chap's difficulties as you are. You will let him stay, won't you, Ned? It is, after all, my fault."

"I'm not so sure of the prudence of his staying here," replied the earl soberly. "I must tell you that my betrothal to his sister is at an end, and his family might not like that he should remain here. He may only be allowed to stay on the understanding that he notifies Lady Jennifer of his whereabouts. I will not have it thought that he's absconded while searches are made for him, and he must return home in time for the holidays."

Throughout the discourse Caesar had been watching all with an extremely intelligent eye and thought it about time the earl be repaid for his kindness. To this end, he reared himself up and, placing his front paws on the coverlet, attempted to lever himself up onto the bed.

"Down, sir," commanded the earl. "You may have won your case to remain in my house, but you will not inhabit my bed. Away with you." Turning a stern countenance toward his brother, he ordered, "If it's your intention to keep the brute, Perry, I suggest you take him to the stables and give him a bath. I will not tolerate the odor of the kennels in my bedchamber."

Undaunted, Peregrine gave a wide grin. "I'm so glad you're home, Ned. Don't know what we would've done without you."

"You will be less than grateful for my return if you don't get that animal out of my room." Suddenly exhaustion overcame him. The day had taken its toll, and he lay back upon his pillows, his countenance paler than ever.

Perry started forward, alarmed at the sudden change. "I say, Ned, you all right? Can I get you anything?"

"Nothing. Nothing. I'm fine. I need to rest, that's all. Now go. I shall do well enough."

With lagging steps, Perry made his way out of the room, finding it necessary to keep checking over his shoulder that his brother was indeed only tired. As he reached the door, he took one final look before entering the corridor and, calling quietly to Caesar, headed toward the stairs to join his friend in the kitchen to sample Rose's cooking.

As December neared its conclusion, Lady Flora Carlton, a small, vivacious brunet dressed in the height of fashion, arrived at Fly around midday to be informed that her brothers had taken a walk to the stables.

"That is no problem," she assured Croft. "If you would but arrange for my trunks to be taken to my old room, I will make myself comfortable in the small salon until they return."

"You intend to stay, madam?" inquired a mystified Croft.

"I do indeed. I will not have it said that I neglect my brother when he has so much need of me. I've told Carlton not to look for my return. I will nurse my dear Edward."

"The master needs no nursemaid, Miss Flora," Croft retorted with a familiarity born of long association. "He does very well. Indeed, he's much improved."

Lady Flora looked contemptuously at the retainer. "When I want your opinion, Croft, I will ask for it. Until then, you may rely upon me to know what's best for my dear brother. I alone shall tend him."

"You mark my words, he'll have none of your 'tending.'

He's no need for petticoats," Croft, muttered, sotto voce, as he went out to the steps to supervise the lady's luggage.

Lady Flora looked fondly around the small salon as she sat sipping her tea. She loved the antiquity of this old house. Although, upon the event of her marriage, she'd been conveyed to Ravensby Hall, at times she still longed for the familiarity of her former home. She had been in Lancashire when news eventually reached her of Edward's return to England, and she begged her husband to conclude his business as quickly as possible so that she could leave for Fly Hall. Seeing the retraction in the *Gazette* made her even more determined to hurry to the earl's side, not wishing him to be alone in what she perceived as his hour of disappointment. Upon her return from Lancashire, she but waited to supervise the Christmas Day festivities at Ravensby before hastening to Fly.

She heard voices in the hall and, putting aside her cup, rose to her feet in anticipation of her brothers' arrival. As Sinclair entered the room, the sight of him affected her deeply, and she ran forward to cast herself, sobbing, onto his breast.

Standing uncertainly in the doorway, Perry looked decidedly uneasy at Flora's show of sisterly concern. Relieved that he was not the recipient of such feminine emotion, he silently sympathized with his brother.

"My dear Flora, there's no need for tears. None at all," said the earl, laughing and attempting to hold her away from him. "As you see, I do very well."

"Your poor arm," she said, fluttering her hand over the empty sleeve, and she was again shaken by a fresh bout of weeping.

"I've told you, I do very well, Flora," stated Sinclair, finally disengaging himself from her clasp. "There is absolutely no need for you to be so distressed on my account." He patted her shoulder reassuringly. "Does Carlton accompany you?" he asked, looking around the room.

Eyes awash with tears, Flora sniffed inelegantly. "I've left him at home; I come to nurse you, to be with you in your time of need."

" 'Nurse' me? I can assure you, my dear, I am in no need of a nurse. Behold, do I seem a man who needs coddling?"

"Wretch!" she cried, stamping her foot. "When I heard of your injuries, I was beside myself. I couldn't bear the thought of your wounds. Now you mock my regard."

"I say, steady on, Flora," cried Perry, stepping forward. "Hasn't Ned enough to contend with without you flying off into one of your starts?"

"Enough! Enough!" cried the earl, raising his hand. "I am gratified by this excessive concern on my behalf, but I assure you, there is no need. Indeed, I am exceedingly pleased to see you, Flora, and should you wish to stay for a little while, I would be more than grateful for your company. However, now that I am returned home, I improve daily and have little use for a nurse. Now come and tell me, how fares Carlton?"

Much mollified by his change of address, Flora took hold of his hand and led him to the chaise, ever eager to chatter on a subject so close to her heart.

Finding himself ignored, Perry decided to make good his escape, quietly calling Caesar to his side and muttering, "Never could understand females. Well, not that one!"

Once the subject of her husband had been exhausted, Flora took the opportunity to raise the subject of the betrothal.

"I had not thought Jenny so cruel as to reject you at such a time," she said reprovingly. "Not at all what I would have expected from her."

"You must not lay the blame at Jenny's door," replied the earl quietly.

Flora came upright in her seat, casting her brother a look of incredulity. "What? I cannot believe it was you who ended the engagement."

"It ended by mutual agreement. We had grown apart."

"Then I can see it was your fault," she said with scorn. "You should have made more of an effort to attach her. You cannot expect to leave a young girl waiting on your return from war without some attempt on your behalf to maintain her interest.

You are my brother, and I love you dearly, but I'm only too aware of your defects. You have no romantic turn of mind whatsoever. I have seen many of society's beauties setting their caps at you, and you took none seriously. You made no endeavor to set up a relationship. I lose all patience with you!"

"Read me no lectures, Flora," he said wearily. "I've no mind to be considering the state of matrimony. Besides, who would have me?"

"I would have expected that Jenny would. At least, she gave me no reason to suspect otherwise."

He rose impatiently. "Then I would not wish myself upon her. I've more sense than that. Now if you will excuse me, I will go to my chamber to change for supper. Might I suggest you do the same?"

Lady Flora's visit became a protracted one. So long was she away that her husband found it necessary to come in search of her.

" 'Tis most unkind of you to expect me to desert my dear Edward," she complained, turning a pouting countenance toward her long-suffering spouse as they sat on the chaise in the morning room. "I've been out of your sight for no more than three weeks, and you find it necessary to seek me out. I am mortified."

"Come, Flora, you would've been even more mortified had I left you to your own devices," cajoled Lord Carlton, a floridly handsome man of middle years who doted unashamedly on his young, effervescent wife. "Admit it—you would rather I missed you than have no care of your whereabouts."

"You are quite right, my love," she agreed penitently. "I would so much rather you sought my company, and I have indeed missed you."

With an indulgent chuckle, he raised her hand to his lips. "You know exactly how to manipulate me. I came here full of righteous indignation at your desertion, and still you find a way of turning it to your advantage."

"I'm so pleased you came," she said, bending forward to

place a kiss on his cheek, but as he would have drawn her into his arms, she braced her hands against his chest. "You must see that I need to be with Edward. I could not rest if I were not."

"I am sure Edward is quite able to care for himself. It is I who have need of you."

She appeared much pleased by this answer and allowed her husband to catch her to his breast, but when they drew apart, she was still reluctant to relinquish her cause.

"Though he will not admit it, I fear Edward is much downcast. Physically, he improves daily, but I fear his spirits do not revive as one would expect. I've a mind to invite him to accompany us to London at the beginning of the season in the hope it might prove a diversion."

"Do you think it would serve?" asked Carlton. "He's been through much, and to expect him to rally too soon could have an adverse effect. Perhaps he would be better waiting until the season is well under way, and his arrival would draw less attention."

"Perhaps you are right," agreed Flora after a moment's thought. "He was ever a favorite among the hostesses, so one need not fear that he would be overlooked."

A clock chiming on the mantel brought her to sudden recollection. "It's five, and they will be returning for tea. We can put it to him then." Almost as an afterthought she added, "You will stay and bear us company, won't you, my love? Perry returns to Oxford, and I would not leave dear Edward alone just yet. Oh, and I must tell you, Perry has acquired the most amusing dog. A real clown, very friendly but quite uncontrollable. Although I cannot help but hope he takes it back with him. I would not have it that he leaves it here."

At that moment the aforesaid animal found it necessary to burst its way into the room and deposit its length before the hearth, its master following in its wake along with his brother.

Smiling, the earl came forward, his hand extended in welcome. "My dear Carlton, 'tis exceedingly good to see you."

Carlton returned his brother-in-law's firm grip and grinned in return. "You may be less than pleased when you know that

I've been commanded to stay," he said. "I trust it finds favor with you, or do you feel you are being invaded? If you do, I swear I will go."

"Not a bit of it," replied the earl. "Though I must tell you that, contrary to my esteemed sister's belief, I don't need to be constantly attended by members of my family. I do very well. Perhaps you can help me to persuade her that I am quite able to continue as normal."

"A chap should be allowed his independence," agreed Carlton. "But perhaps, if you have no objections, we should stay for a few days more, if only to make our minds easy on the score."

The maid entered with the tea tray, and when she withdrew, they all settled themselves comfortably by the fire while Flora attended to the filling of the cups.

"If you've a mind to stay, perhaps you would like to cast your eye over some of the young stock in the stables," said the earl. "There's a particular piece of blood I wouldn't mind bringing on. Excellent conformation and showing some spirit . . ."

"Edward! You are not to be thinking of horses," remonstrated Flora. "In your state of health . . ."

Sinclair cast her a scornful glance. "My dear sister, are you proposing that I walk for the rest of my life? It's only my arm that's missing, nothing else, and with a little modification to the aids, I shall manage very well, thank you. You must become reconciled to the fact that I intend to recommence my life as normal. I am no puling invalid who needs to be forever fussed over."

Flora bridled, her displeasure showing in every line. "Obviously! Then perhaps you would prefer it if Carlton and I return home, and then you can do whatever you please without having us worry over you."

"That's hardly called for," interpolated Perry, hastening to his brother's defense. "You know as well as I, that isn't what Ned meant. You smother him, Flora. You must allow him some freedom."

"Peace! Peace!" cried the earl, raising his hand to silence his siblings. "I am extremely grateful for your concerns on my behalf and promise not to attempt anything that might jeopardize my recovery. Will that suffice? Do I now find favor with you?"

"You always do," said a penitent Flora. "Indeed, 'tis only our affection for you that prompts our concern."

"Then, my dear sister, you will find me ever mindful of your wishes."

"Faradiddle!" was her unconvinced reply as she confined her attentions to refilling her cup.

Chapter Three

London in season was a veritable hive of entertainment, and Lady Jennifer Lynton cast herself into the midst of the gaiety with enthusiasm, no amusement seeming beneath her notice. Indeed, she appeared tireless, and it was the common consensus that she had recovered admirably from what was termed her "disappointment." She had a refreshing naïvete about her that appealed to both hostesses and guests alike, ensuring she spent very few nights at home, this being the first season she had experienced without the restraints of a betrothal.

However, entertaining her would-be sister-in-law one fine afternoon, she found it difficult to keep her equanimity on the subject of engagements. Miss Amelia Cheviot was a young lady with such a directness of manner and soberness of demeanor that Jennifer often wondered at her brother's desire to take her to wife. However, while she bore no great liking for her, she attempted to tolerate her company as best she might. To that end, she offered to accompany her on an expedition to choose the material for her new ball gown, and upon their return they repaired to the small salon for refreshments.

Miss Cheviot eyed her companion from beneath lowered lashes as they sat taking tea. "My dear Jenny," she said, "I could scarcely believe my ears when dearest Arthur told me that you refused to reconsider your rejection of Sinclair."

"I have no desire whatsoever to be married," said Jennifer in a tone she hoped would bring about a speedy end to the unwelcome turn in conversation.

However, Miss Cheviot had no intention of relinquishing her cause so easily. "I'm sure that can't be true. Why, surely 'tis every girl's dream to be married, and to such a personable gentleman too. It's rumored that his income alone is . . ."

Jennifer could not believe her companion's temerity in pursuing the topic. "I care not what his income may be. If I marry, it will certainly not be for consideration of my husband's wealth. I have sufficient of my own to render such mercenary thoughts unnecessary."

"Then if it's for the loss of his arm . . ."

"It most certainly is not the loss of his arm, and I find it less than charitable of you to mention it. Why, the loss of his arm can in no way detract from his person. Indeed, I had not even given it a thought."

"Then there's no reason on this earth you should not reconsider the betrothal," said Miss Cheviot with obvious satisfaction.

Jenny rose hastily to her feet. "It is sufficient," she said, attempting to retain her composure, "that I have to contend with my brother forever badgering me to marry, without your joining his ranks. I am well aware of your desire to remove me from this house, but you may tell Arthur that you have failed in your mission."

Miss Cheviot had the grace to blush, "I assure you, dear Jennifer . . ." she began, but words failed her at the look of scorn that crossed her companion's countenance.

"There's no need for you to make avowals that are blatantly untrue, Amelia. I am well aware that my continued presence becomes an embarrassment to you both, but I warn you that you must bear it as best you may. I have no intention of marrying for your convenience." Without looking back, Jenny left the room; it would not do to stay, lest her companion became aware of the hurt she felt.

"Well!" expostulated Miss Cheviot to the empty room. "Well!"

The Duchess of Rye's ball was hailed as one of the main events of the season. The splendid rooms of Rye House had been transformed into temples of old Rome, and even the servants wore togas for the occasion. Magnificent dishes were laid out in the supper room, where a small fountain flowed with wine.

No matter how magnificent the occasion, however, Jennifer found no delight in having to accompany her brother and his affianced. Indeed, she would have much preferred to remain at home, but to refuse the invitation would appear churlish. She had resisted the temptation to dress as a Roman goddess, as had so many of the other ladies present, preferring instead to wear a gown of ivory silk adorned with knots of gold-spangled ribbon.

Nevertheless, once the Earl of Hawley's party arrived in the ballroom, it was not long before Lady Jennifer became the center of a small group of admirers, each eager to attract her attention. However, it was to the young Lord Melville that she finally granted the first dance, and he eagerly led her onto the floor as the strains of the orchestra heralded a cotillion. Lord Melville proved an engaging partner, his bantering conversation keeping her amused throughout the movements, and when, at its end, he offered to find her refreshment, she had no hesitation whatsoever in accepting.

So engrossed was she in watching the progress of those engaged in the current set of country dances that she failed to notice her escort's return. However, she was visibly startled when, taking his seat beside her, he bent close to whisper into her ear, and it took a moment before she could take in what he was saying.

"My dear Lady Jennifer," whispered Lord Melville, drawing

his seat closer still, "I hope you will not find it indelicate of me, but I must make you aware that Sinclair is here. Indeed, he draws quite a crowd. So many are there who are eager to welcome his return that he is positively surrounded with well-wishers."

For a moment she turned startled eyes to his face but soon recovered, not wishing to seem in any way perturbed. She smiled, attempting the ordinary. "His return is of no consequence to me. I assure you, I find his comings and goings no matter for comment. Indeed, if I should never set eyes on the man again, I will not feel his loss."

Much heartened by this response, Lord Melville proceeded to attempt to divert his companion with the latest morsels of gossip, oblivious to the emotions his words had evoked in her breast.

As the evening advanced and the earl had still not seen fit to seek her out, Jennifer's mood became one of forced indifference, and she entered into the spirit of the evening with much enthusiasm. However, in a quiet moment, when she had removed herself to a seat by an open casement, eager to feel its cooling breeze, she became aware that she was the object of scrutiny.

Turning in her chair, she saw the earl, elegant in evening attire, standing but a few feet away, conversing with one of his cronies. If not for the loss of his arm and the pale scar that now creased his left cheek, Jennifer would not have believed him returned from war. He retained his noble grace and bearing, appearing oblivious to the interest he evoked, and she could easily believe that he would once more become the darling of the London hostesses.

As he excused himself from his companion, she saw that he intended to advance toward her, and she immediately rose to leave.

"What, you would desert me, Lady Jennifer?" he said, smiling as he came to stand before her. "Am I not to be allowed at least one word with you?"

"I am totally out of patience with you, my lord, and have no desire whatsoever to talk to you," she snapped, resuming her seat and refusing to meet his gaze.

At her attempt to rebuff him, he stood squarely before her. "Come, Jenny, it must not be seen that we argue and feed the scandalmongers. At least among company it must seem that we can be civil to each other. Think of the attention we would draw if we appear antagonistic." As she gave no answer, he drew up a chair to sit beside her. Concern showing on his handsome countenance, he laid his hand over hers as it rested in her lap.

"Would you have it said that there is a bitterness between us?" he asked quietly, attempting to read her face. "*Is* there a bitterness between us?"

Still she made no reply, and he pressed the hand that he held. "I see that I have wounded you, but believe me when I say that it is for the best. You would not wish me to be your husband. Come, did we not agree to at least be friends? I wish not to alienate you."

Jennifer still gave no immediate reply. But then, raising her eyes to his face, she smiled and said, "Yes, I do believe we may suit as friends. Though what society will make of us, I know not."

"Do you care what the tabbies say?"

She gave a small trill of amusement. "Not in the least, sir."

"Good," he said, rising from his seat. "Perhaps now that our friendship is confirmed, you might consider using my given name, for, as you may have noticed, I have every intention of using yours." He bowed formally and held out his hand. "Would you do me the honor of standing up with me for this waltz? I do believe we may attempt it in all propriety."

"But how, Edward?" she asked, for a fleeting moment allowing her eyes to glance at his left shoulder.

"Pay no mind to that, my dear. I do believe that with a little ingenuity we will manage quite creditably. You need only rest your hand on my shoulder, and all will work out perfectly."

She appeared taken aback by the suggestion. "I could not, sir. It would look almost as if we embraced, and as we are no longer betrothed, it would appear quite shocking. Even if we were, it would cause comments."

He grinned at the idea, his eyes dancing with devilment. "I'd not thought of it. Yes, I can quite see that we would cause a stir, but I do believe that we really must. Let the tabbies say what they like. I must have you dance with me."

She smiled, an answering sparkle in her eyes. "Then, sir, dance with you I will. I care not for the scandalmongers. I'm quite sure your impeccable reputation will more than render us immune to their malicious gossip."

"Is my reputation impeccable?" he asked with some surprise.

"Most certainly! Especially as you are one of the gallant few who are returned victorious from war."

"What utter nonsense," he scoffed, laughing. "I assure you, there's nothing gallant about war."

Taking her hand in a firm clasp, he led her determinedly onto the dance floor, and as they began the movements, they became aware that several pairs of curious eyes followed their progress around the room. At first his movements felt awkward, but soon he relaxed and followed the familiar rhythm of the dance, his right arm snugly encircling Jennifer's slender waist. It felt so right, and soon they were oblivious to the interest they evoked, only aware of their enjoyment of the moment and each other's company.

Reaching scarcely above Sinclair's shoulder, Jennifer stole a glance up at her partner's countenance to find him watching her intently, an unfathomable look in his storm-gray eyes. When she would have queried that look, he swept her into a series of intricate moves, from which they emerged breathless and laughing.

Once the dance ended, Sinclair still retained his hold on her hand as they returned to the seat by the window. He smiled, handing her to her chair as he scanned the onlookers for signs of disapproval. "We appear to have escaped censure for the moment, but now I will leave you before I render our reputations beyond repair."

As he bowed over her hand, her fingers clung for a moment to his, and he raised an inquiring eyebrow.

"I forget," she said, smiling. "I must thank you for allowing Freddie to stay with you last term. Arthur would have berated him terribly if he'd known that he'd been rusticated."

"He still does not know?"

"No, and I would be grateful if you would not mention the matter to him."

"Nothing would induce me to, my dear. It was naught but a boyish prank instigated by Perry and his hapless hound. Freddie but championed them. Do not fear, I've already read them a lecture on the subject and extracted a promise for more decorum in the future."

She laughed. "No matter what lectures you make, I can hardly see those two behaving with decorum."

Sinclair smiled in agreement. "Neither can I, but an attempt must be made to instill at least some sense into their nonsensical brains."

At that moment, they spied Lady Flora bearing down upon them, a young debutante in her wake.

"Oh, Lord, not Flora with one of her *hopefuls* again," groaned the earl. "She's forever trotting them out for my inspection. She still holds hopes that eventually one will catch my eye."

"And will one?" asked Jennifer coldly.

"Never!" he replied with determination, and, once more bowing, he relinquished her company and prepared for his sister's onslaught.

Viewing the earl's departure from the alcove where he'd been waiting, Lord Melville immediately returned to Jenny's side. However, his joy at reclaiming her company was short-lived, as he was met with a frosty reception and soon found it necessary to seek out his cronies in the card room.

When news that Lady Jennifer Lynton and the Earl of Sinclair had enjoyed a cozy tête-à-tête and even waltzed together at the duchess' ball permeated society, they found themselves the object of speculation and their movements commented on whenever they ventured forth to an event.

So out of patience did Jennifer become with the comments she frequently overheard, she decided to turn her energies in a completely different direction, eager for a diversion from Sinclair. To that end she commissioned her brother to purchase a high-perch phaeton for her. It had long been her ambition to tool such a vehicle, and this seemed an excellent opportunity to achieve it.

When approached on the subject, Hawley was not in agreement with her scheme, saying with a great deal of censure that no lady of quality would be seen driving such a sporting vehicle. That, however, only served to strengthen her resolve that no other conveyance would suffice, and to that end she engaged the services of a reputable coach builder. Within a short space of time she contracted to purchase a very smart phaeton with double perches of swan-neck pattern and eagerly awaited its arrival. Being presented with a fait accompli, Hawley, very much against his better judgment, eventually agreed to visit Tattersall's in an attempt to purchase a pair of suitable horses.

Upon his return he proudly informed her that he'd managed to acquire a pair of very sweet-goers, even if at one stage he'd been in danger of being outbid by the Duke of Cumberland's agent.

In less than a week the sight of Lady Jennifer Lynton driving a fine pair of grays with a liveried groom perched behind her became a familiar sight in town.

Driving down Bond Street one sunny afternoon on her way to the park, she noticed the Earl of Sinclair leaving one of the shops and setting out on foot toward his club. Bringing her horses to a halt, she ordered the groom to their heads and waited at the roadside for his approach. However, he appeared oblivious to her presence as he closely inspected something in his hand and almost passed the vehicle without noticing it.

"Edward!" she cried in a reproving voice, and immediately he turned to face her, slipping the article hastily into his pocket.

Making a slight bow, he smiled and approached the side of the vehicle, flicking his eyes over the equipage. "Lady Jennifer and her grays," he said, humor in his voice. "You set the town on its ears, my dear. I wonder at your daring."

"Edward, if you intend to find fault with me, I will have none of you," she said, feigning hauteur and taking the reins in both hands as if to move off.

Bowing slightly, the earl mastered his amusement. "Not at all, Jenny. I wholeheartedly approve of your spirit of adventure."

She looked a challenge at him. "Then will you prove your approbation by sitting up with me? I am headed for the park. That is, if you will trust me to drive you."

He grinned openly. "From what I've heard of your skill with the ribbons, I certainly need have no fear of sitting up with you. But do you think it wise that I accompany you and feed the gossips?"

"If it is your fear that we feed the gossips, then no more need be said," she said, nodding to the groom to resume his seat as she prepared to move forward.

"Nothing of the sort." The earl grinned, stepping nimbly up to sit beside her. "If you can brave the stares we will inevitably create, then so can I."

"It's uncommon to find you on foot at this time of day," she commented as they drove in the direction of Hyde Park. "Were you on some errand? What was it that you hid so quickly in your pocket? A *billet-doux* from a sweetheart?"

"Certainly not," he answered with amusement. "I have to admit, 'tis naught but a trifle."

"May I see this trifle?" she asked, curious.

"I assure you, 'tis nothing that would interest you. I but collected a miniature I had had reframed," he explained. "The original was accidentally scorched by a candle."

"Who is it a portrait of?" she asked, not daring to take her eyes off the road in the press of vehicles that milled in the busy London streets.

"My grandsire," he replied with aplomb.

"Oh," she replied, losing all interest in the subject.

Their drive around the park was punctuated by many curious stares, some pedestrians actually standing agape as Jennifer drove the grays at a spanking trot around the park's perimeter. One hopeful even stated to his companions, "Mark my words, they'll make a match of it yet. I'll lay you a monkey on it."

However, if he'd been aware of the turn of conversation taking place in the phaeton, he would have been less than sure.

"Has Melville made you an offer of marriage yet?" asked the earl, watching from beneath lowered eyebrows for her reaction.

"Good heavens, no," replied Jenny with some surprise. "Indeed he has not. Whatever made you suppose such a thing?"

"He will. You mark my words. . . ."

"Then I will leave him in no uncertainty of my feelings on the matter."

"Which are?"

"You are insufferable, Edward. I've no desire whatsoever to marry Melville!"

He chuckled. "Not even when he pays you such marked attention?"

"Most certainly not."

"Ah, then his heart will be broken!"

"His purse, more likely. I am well aware that my fortune is where my attraction lies."

He looked at her sharply. "I hope you will not judge everyone by that standard, my dear."

"I've had no reason to revise my judgment," she answered sharply, and, turning the vehicle, she headed out of the park.

A few days later Lady Flora found it necessary to take her brother to task as they sat over supper at Sinclair House, the earl's London residence.

"I've been out of town but a week, Edward," she said curtly, "and the first thing I hear on my return is that you've been seen driving with Jennifer. In the park, if you please. I don't know what ails the pair of you. First there was the betrothal, then the rejection, and now you seem forever in each other's pocket. Exactly what is afoot?"

"I don't know your meaning," he replied, confining his attention to refilling his glass. "Are we not now allowed to continue as friends? Must something be read into our every movement?"

"When you feed the gossipmongers, what else do you expect? She has a fortune almost to compare with your own, which she inherited from her mother's side of the family. In common with any other heiress, her actions must cause comment. Surely you must see that you will be observed." Fearing that her words made no impression on her brother, Flora redoubled her efforts. "Do you think you can play fast and loose with each other without raising interest? I am quite out of patience with both of you."

"Then you need not be. If you think I draw too much attention to us, I will attempt to avoid her company. I would not wish it to be thought that I prevent eligible suitors from presenting themselves."

"That's not at all what I meant, and you know it," said Flora contritely, "but I would ask if you have an interest in the child. Do you regret the break? Is there hope of a reconciliation?"

"No, there is not," he replied tersely, pushing his chair from the table and rising. "Must I keep repeating to you that I will *never* marry?"

"Then, Edward, you are a bigger fool than I gave you credit for. Surely you do not intend to remain unwed. If nothing else, think of the title!"

"Perry shall remain my heir, and he need have no reservations about marrying. Have no fear, the title will not die out. Does that satisfy you?"

Flora visibly blanched at this onslaught. "That's not at all what I meant. . . ." But whatever else she would have said was lost as Sinclair strode from the room, leaving her to continue her meal alone.

When next the much-observed couple met, it was at a musical evening arranged by Lord and Lady Clay at their elegant town house. A quintet and a fashionable songstress had been hired for the occasion, and the stylish rooms were ablaze with light and filled with the cream of London society.

It was only at Flora's instigation that Sinclair accepted the invitation to the event. He bore no great liking for such entertainment, finding the music thought suitable on such occasions not at all to his taste.

However, arriving just as the quintet began their recital, he was obliged to sit well to the rear of the room and was therefore able to observe Jennifer for quite some time before she became aware of his presence during the supper interval.

Mindful of his sister's words, he did not immediately seek her out. Instead, he merely nodded briefly in her direction when she became aware of his presence.

Jennifer was accompanied by Lord Melville, and when she caught the earl's eye, she cast him a meaningful look. If in that moment she appeared merrier and more pleased with her escort than she had for the previous part of the evening, who was to censure her? Certainly not Melville! He found her change in mood most encouraging.

Seeing that Sinclair had no intention of approaching her, Jenny became more determined to show her indifference to his actions, while the whole room waited with bated breath for the couple's response to the encounter.

However, society was doomed to disappointment. If they were hoping to witness any dialogue between the pair, they were sadly mistaken. Both appeared indifferent to the other's actions.

Lady Clay was heard to comment on dear Jennifer's vivacity, but, apart from that, there was no further cause for comment. When, at the end of the evening, the two guests left without as much as a glance in the other's direction, none could fault their conduct.

Returning to his lodgings some while later, Lord Melville congratulated himself on the outcome of the evening, believing that at last he appeared to be making some progress with the young heiress.

Jennifer, however, viewed the event quite differently. Sitting before her dressing-table mirror, she dismissed her maid. "Insufferable man," she declared to the pale little face that looked back at her. "I care not if I should never see him again." And who knew whether she spoke of Melville or Sinclair, for even she did not!

The earl also repaired to his apartment at Fly Hall in no even frame of mind, but when he opened the drawer to his dresser and saw the portrait gazing back at him from its new frame, his expression softened, and all irritation left him.

As the season advanced, society ceased to be forever expectant of a reconciliation between Sinclair and Lady Jennifer. Some young bucks were even prepared to speculate as to which of their numbers would succeed in securing the lady's hand. It was noticeable, however, that she treated them all with the same open friendliness, showing no partiality whatsoever to any one of them.

The Earl of Hawley had been obliged to reject no fewer than four applications for her hand and was becoming increasingly incensed with her blank refusal to even contemplate matrimony, believing her stubbornness to be nothing more than an attempt to thwart his own plans to enter the married state. So uncomfortable became the atmosphere when they met in the dining room that Jennifer attempted to avoid the encounters, preferring to eat in her apartment on the rare occasion when Hawley dined at home.

Chapter Four

To Flora's annoyance, Sinclair appeared to be losing interest in society, finding it necessary to refuse what she thought of as perfectly suitable invitations—invitations that at any other time he would delight in accepting—preferring instead to remain at Sinclair House or to visit one or two of the select clubs to which he belonged.

Although she made known her disapproval, she could not help but feel for her brother. Nevertheless, when an invitation came from Major Drake to join him and fellow officers for a reunion supper in Richmond, she found he needed no encouragement to accept. He set forth with some enthusiasm, evidently eager, after so lengthy a break, to meet with the other officers of his regiment on the rare occasion of their being granted furlough.

The evening had advanced into the small hours of the morning when finally Edward's coach returned home. The slight rolling of his gait proclaimed his inebriation as, entering the hallway, he presented the attending footman with his hat and cane.

"There's a young gentleman waiting for you in the library, my lord," confided the footman. "He arrived about midnight."

"My brother?" asked the earl, a bemused frown clouding his brow.

"No, sir. He gave his name as the Honorable Frederick Lynton. I told him you were not at home, but he insisted that he wait for you."

"What now?" groaned the earl, feeling in that moment un-equal to the task of entering into a conversation that would tax his ingenuity. It was with some effort that he turned toward the library when he so much would have preferred to retire to his bed.

The candles had burned low in the sconces, casting the room deeply into shadow. When the earl entered, he was sur-prised to see the youth lying with his head on his arms at the desk, obviously asleep. As he approached, Freddie mumbled inaudibly and moved his head slightly so that one arm hid his face. Sinclair halted his progress. There was something not quite right about the form before him. It had the same dark, curly hair, but there was something about the set of the shoul-ders. . . . They were far too slim. Indeed, the whole upper part of the body appeared too slight.

Confused, he sat heavily in the leather chair set before the desk and attempted to force his eyes to focus on the boy be-fore him. He cursed the fact that he'd drunk so much wine and shook his head as if to rid himself of its effects, but the figure remained the same. There was definitely something odd about the boy.

Due to the lateness of the hour and his intoxicated state, as he relaxed in the chair, his head drooped forward, and he, too, drifted into sleep. However, after only a few moments, an in-sistent hand shaking his shoulder woke him, and with a great effort he fought his way back to consciousness.

"Edward, do wake up," commanded an urgent voice. "I have need of you! Wake up!"

"Jen?" he expostulated in a bewildered tone, attempting to focus on the face above him.

"You're drunk!" she accused with disgust.

"No, I'm not foxed," he corrected, straightening in his seat. "Just slightly bosky."

"You are decidedly drunk. I can't believe you would choose this of all nights."

"My profound apologies," he said, gripping her shoulder and rising unsteadily to his feet. "Bad form to be bamboozled in front of a lady." His eyes narrowed as he took stock of the figure before him. "What's happened to your hair, Jen, and why are you wearing boy's clothes? Though I must say, they suit you admirably." Then, almost as an afterthought, he asked, "Are they Freddie's?"

"Yes, but never mind that," she said impatiently, pushing him back into his seat. "Do try to understand that I need you."

"At your service," he said, once more standing erect and bowing. "I'm not so bosky as to render me useless, but I feel I must point out to you, my dear, that I am not at my best, and this situation is highly irregular." A frown puckered his brow as he looked questioningly about the room. "Does your maid accompany you? I don't see her, and surely you must realize that to be visiting a bachelor's establishment at this time of night, and without even your maid, is not at all the thing."

She looked impatiently at him. "No, no one accompanies me. Oh, do sit down, Edward. I can't talk to you when you tower over me as you're doing now."

"Why *are* you here?" he asked, resuming his seat. As an afterthought, he added, "Not run away, have you?"

"Certainly not! Though, upon reflection, I can see that it may seem that I have. I never thought of it in that light. Now it will not do that you sidetrack me. It's Perry and that ungracious brother of mine."

He groaned, putting his hand to his bowed head. "Not another scrape! What now?"

"Perry came to see me late this afternoon. Freddie's absconded."

"What the deuce for? Why did Perry not come to me?"

"He said that you were away from home, and he'd tried to sort the matter out on his own, but now that Freddie's gone, he had to come to tell me."

"What the devil is all this about—another prank?"

"It's slightly more serious than a prank this time. A fight."

"A fight?" he repeated stupidly, sitting fully erect and giving her the whole of his attention.

"They stole out after hours to go to a cockfight that had been arranged in a local barn, and there were quite a few sporting bucks there. Freddie got embroiled in an argument with one of them that resulted in a mill. His opponent fell heavily, striking his head, and lost consciousness. Thinking he'd killed him, Freddie took to his heels before they could call the runners."

"Stupid boy!" remonstrated Sinclair. "And I suppose Perry was no better?"

"Perry went after him to reassure him that his opponent was merely stunned, but he could not find him. When he eventually returned to his rooms, a note had been delivered to say that Freddie was going into hiding and Perry should not try to find him."

"All this would've been totally unnecessary if only they'd come to me," complained the earl, sighing heavily with frustration. "Though where to start to look for him, I don't know."

"I do," she said with some aplomb, "but I can't go alone. Therefore, so as not to involve anyone else in the matter, I've decided that you will take me. I've told Perry to stay here, should Freddie return while we are away. We must travel incognito, of course, which is why I dress as a boy. It would cause too much comment if you were seen to be accompanied by a girl. . . ."

"And it would not draw interest and comment if you are seen in the company of a one-armed man?" he asked scornfully. "We could hardly go unnoticed."

"Now you are being difficult. I've thought of that. We shall travel on the Accommodation Coach as . . . brothers, or cousins, or even tutor and pupil. We are less likely to be noticed if we travel on a public conveyance than if we use one of our own vehicles."

"You've thought this out quite thoroughly," he said, slightly surprised and not without admiration. "But there's no need for you to become embroiled in the affair. I will follow in Freddie's wake and bring him back. There's no need for you to be setting out on such a venture."

"There's every need, for I know where to search, and you don't. I couldn't tell Arthur—you must see that. He would berate Freddie shamefully, and who knows what state of mind poor Freddie's in? No, I must go, and if you choose not to accompany me, then so be it."

He saw the impropriety of the situation, but his inebriation made him reckless. However, he made one last attempt to persuade her to remain in London. "I take it that you've left no message for Hawley?"

"No!"

"Then when it is seen that you are gone, it will be thought that you've eloped or some such. Do you think that wise?"

"Wise or not, there's no alternative. Edward, *do* hurry," she pleaded, taking hold of his sleeve. "We don't have much time if we are to catch the Accommodation Coach; it leaves The Blue Boar for Coventry at five."

"Where are we heading?"

"Buxton in Derbyshire."

"Why in the devil's name Buxton? Its halfway up the country!"

"Because I believe Freddie will have gone to an old friend who lives there, and, of course, he will think that Buxton is far enough away to be of no interest to the runners."

"You realize, of course, that, being somewhat in my cups, I will probably regret this in the morning," he warned, standing and making for the door. "We can't set out totally unprepared. I will put some necessary items into a valise. I trust you've not come empty-handed?"

She looked meaningfully toward a small cloak bag that had remained unnoticed by the hearth.

When he returned to the library a short while later, he'd changed his evening clothes for the more serviceable attire of buckskin breeches with top boots and a coat of dark blue superfine.

Jennifer darted from the chair where she'd been waiting impatiently for his return. "Thank goodness you've come," she said a little breathlessly. "I was beginning to despair and thought you had fallen asleep."

"Never!" he replied, making a small bow. "Would I do such a thing when a lady is waiting for me?"

She cast him a deprecating glance. "Edward, am I to get *any* sense from you?" she asked.

"I'd thought I was all sense," he replied, grinning down at her. "See? I even remembered the money." And he held out his wallet as proof.

"I've been thinking about that," she said soberly. "I've a notion the amount of money I have in my purse will not suffice. Therefore, I would be grateful if you would keep a strict tally on what you are obliged to spend on my behalf, and I will ensure you are repaid on our return."

"Then I shall be banker. Though, as for keeping tally, I must warn you that I can be quite unreliable in that direction. There's absolutely no need to keep account of my expenditure on your behalf, as I will bear whatever costs are necessary. Now we must go before the servants start to stir. The hall porter has retired, so if we make haste, we may leave unobserved."

Within a short while of leaving the yard at The Blue Boar, the rocking of the coach lulled Sinclair into a deep slumber from which it would have taken nothing short of an explosion to wake him. Surprisingly, there had been few passengers awaiting the coach, and he'd been able to secure a window seat with Jennifer sitting between him and a clerical gentleman who was equally eager to seek repose. Sitting opposite them was a rotund man of uncertain occupation who insisted upon attempting to engage Jennifer in conversation, his wife, punctuating each of his sentences with a nod of her head, seemingly just as eager to set up a dialogue.

Feeling unequal to a lively tête-à-tête so early in the day, Jennifer gave only monosyllabic replies before stating herself to be extremely tired and, begging her companions' pardon, rested her head against Sinclair's shoulder, and she, too, drifted into sleep.

Several changes of teams were achieved at the coaching inns en route before she again woke to find her traveling companions to have changed. The cleric remained, but the opposite seat now contained two birdlike spinsters who were obviously sisters and an elderly gentleman who appeared to be in their care, as they constantly fussed over him.

Relinquishing her position against Sinclair's shoulder, she sat erect, casting him a sidelong glance that assured her he still slumbered. To her vast amusement, his curly-brimmed beaver was now set at a rakish angle over one eye, and she fought the impulse to issue a very unladylike giggle.

"Have you enjoyed your sleep, young sir?" asked the elderly gentleman, smiling indulgently at her. "I would suppose it was a very early start for such a youngster as yourself."

"Oh, I'm older than I look, sir," she replied, relishing her role of schoolboy.

The elderly man grinned. "And how old might that be? You're naught but a young shaver of a lad."

She thought hurriedly. She'd not given her appearance much thought but realized that, as she wore her brother's earlier schoolboy garb, she must appear to be very young.

"Twelve," she replied with composure, hoping to have chosen correctly.

The old man grinned. "And is this your father, my boy?" he asked, nodding at the earl.

"Certainly not," she replied with some amusement. "He's my tutor, Mr. Thurston."

The old man, who informed her that his name was Griffin

and that he traveled with his daughters, eyed the earl uncertainly, taking in the cut of his coat and the gleam of his top boots. "He's a very elegant-looking tutor. Never known any tutor to wear clothes of that quality." Then, nodding briefly at Sinclair's left shoulder, he observed, "Been in the war, has he?"

"Mr. Thurston likes to dress to perfection," confided Jennifer, sotto voce. "Though I know not how he bears the expense on a tutor's salary. As to the war . . ."

The earl pulled his length upright in the seat and pushed back his beaver from his brow. "Jen . . ." he warned.

Mr. Griffin chuckled. "Jen? Jen? What kind of name is that for a young lad?"

"Jem," corrected Sinclair, suppressing a grin. "Master Jeremiah Scatterwell."

Jennifer shot him a look of horror, thinking the brandy from the previous night must have addled his brain, but, seeing only a gleam of amusement in his eye, she resigned herself to being the recipient of such an ignoble name.

The earl removed his hat, placing it upon one knee, and attempted to straighten his crumpled neck-cloth. It had been a devil of a job to change his clothing unaided the previous night, and it irked him that it had been tied with less than its customary precision, but under the circumstances it was unavoidable. His memory of the event that had led to this highly unconventional journey being somewhat hazy, he attempted to put his thoughts into order. When full recollection came, he pondered the folly of setting out on such a mission. Certainly Freddie needed to be retrieved, but he should have insisted that Jennifer return home and then undertaken the journey alone. He couldn't believe that he'd been so foolish as to have agreed to her impulsive scheme.

When the coach arrived at its next stop and all the passengers alighted to partake of a light luncheon, Sinclair took hold of Jennifer's arm and propelled her toward the inn's private parlor, ordering the landlord to provide a hasty cold collation. As soon as the door closed in the man's wake, he spun her around, a distinct look of indignation on his face.

"Like to 'dress to perfection,' do I? Don't know how I 'bear the expense on a tutor's salary'?" he said. "May I point out to you, young lady, I am no coxcomb. I am known for my moderation in dress."

"If you will insist on traveling in clothes that proclaim the hand of a master tailor, what else could I have said?" she replied defiantly. "Some explanation needed to be given."

Releasing his hold on her arm, he sat on the settle. "Of course you're right," he replied. "Though I'm still not sure how I allowed you to involve me in this escapade in the first place. I am also known as a very rational man, and I can't believe I was so easily persuaded to go against all that is sensible."

"That's quite simple." She chuckled. "You were drunk, but surely you saw that I couldn't travel alone." Then, recollecting the issue, she demanded, "And may I ask why you felt the need to saddle me with the name of Jeremiah Scatterwell?"

Unrepentant, he grinned. "Jeremiah is a very noble name. There had to be some explanation for why I'd called you Jen."

"Does that mean I may now call you Ned, as the boys do?" she asked hopefully.

"No, my lady, it does not. Even a young gentleman as noble as Master Jeremiah Scatterwell would not be allowed to take such liberties with his tutor. It shall be Mr. Thurston. You must treat me with respect."

"Humph," she replied. "And what respect am I due?"

"None whatsoever, my dear. You are reduced to the rank of scrubby schoolboy. 'Twas your idea to masquerade as one, and so you shall be treated."

The entrance of the landlord bearing a tray containing a foaming tankard of ale and a glass of lemonade prevented any further discourse on the subject. His wife, following with a meal of cold meats and bread and butter, smiled briefly in the travelers' direction before dropping a hasty curtsy and withdrawing in her husband's wake.

Jennifer pulled a chair up to the table and forked some beef and pork onto her plate. The lemonade she found quite refreshing, and it was a moment before she realized that the earl watched her from his seat by the hearth, a wealth of amusement evident in his eyes.

"Won't you join me, Edward?" she asked.

Grinning, he held up his hand in reply. "I feel not the need for food at the moment. But please, don't let me spoil your appetite, which appears *quite* in order."

"Of course, I was forgetting your hangover," she replied with disdain.

"I'm never known to suffer the effects of a hangover, my girl. I am merely not hungry."

"You don't fool me, Edward Thurston. Admit it, you're feeling rather green about the gills. I've seen that look often enough when Arthur has overimbibed."

He came and sat at the table and took some of the meats onto his plate. "There, does that satisfy you?" he asked.

"You really should eat something, Edward, for who knows when our next stop will be?"

Having rejoined the coach some short while later, their next stop came rather sooner than they had anticipated. Midway through the afternoon, as they negotiated a sharp bend in the lane, they encountered a young sporting gentleman dashing along in his phaeton, forcing the coach driver to bring his team sharply to the side of the road. Much confusion ensued as the two teams swerved dangerously to avoid a collision, resulting in the coach mounting the bank of a deep ditch and slithering down the other side. Springing his horses and without as much as a backward glance, the gentleman disappeared almost as suddenly as he had materialized.

Everyone inside the coach was thrown heavily to one side, and there were cries and oaths of differing force from its occupants amid the sound of splintering wood and breaking glass. Jennifer felt herself pinioned securely to the earl, his right arm holding her fast against his side.

"Any harm done, Jen?" he asked as she attempted to right herself.

"I'm fine, sir," she replied, then added ruefully, "you cushioned my fall." Her gaze involuntarily went to his left shoulder. "I hope I haven't injured you, Edward. I would never forgive myself. . . ."

"I, too, am fine," he said with a reassuring smile. "Though I don't think Mr. Griffin has fared as well. He appears considerably winded."

The Misses Griffin appeared to be of no use whatsoever in such a situation, one indulging in a fit of hysterics while the other swooned completely away. The cleric however, seemed equal to the task. Pushing open the off-side door, which was now uppermost, he climbed out and, taking hold of Jennifer's hand, pulled her clear of the doorway. Aided by Sinclair from inside the coach, Mr. Griffin, amid much huffing and puffing, was carefully raised aloft, the cleric taking him to sit on the opposite side of the lane away from the vehicle and the unsettled horses.

The coach driver, relinquishing the care of his animals to the guard, came to the opening. "Out with you, sir," he said to the earl, giving him a hand to aid his ascent, then turned to the cleric. "If you would but climb once more into the coach, sir, we can lift the ladies out."

Once the spinsters were retrieved from the coach and been assured that no further danger was likely, they appeared to rally and confined their energies to the care of their father, who also appeared to be recovering from the experience. The coachman, mounting one of the wheelers, declared his intention of riding back to the last coaching inn they had visited to secure another vehicle so that they might continue their journey.

As the afternoon advanced into early evening and dusk began to fall, Jennifer sat with chin in hand on the bank a little way from the rest of the travelers. Standing before her, the earl watched for any sign of the returning coachman, but as none was apparent, he turned to face her.

"I see no point in waiting here longer," he said. "I noticed that we passed a small inn on the road, probably not more than two or three miles back. I think it would be prudent to seek accommodation before our companions have the same idea and all the rooms are spoken for. It would not do that we should be forced to spend the night in the open."

"An excellent idea," agreed Jennifer, coming to her feet and picking up her cloak bag.

Having taken leave of their fellow passengers, who all declared their intention of awaiting the replacement coach, they retraced their steps along the dusty lane.

As they walked, Jennifer examined the earl's profile. "Do you regret setting out with me, Edward?" she asked in a small voice.

"To tell the truth, surprisingly, I do not," he replied, returning her regard and smiling. "I thought at first that I would, but I was quite wrong. Though I know not what they will be thinking in London when our absence is discovered."

"They will think that we've eloped." She giggled, adding a little skip to her step, seemingly amused by the whole idea.

"And that thought does not worry you?"

"Not in the least. They may think what they like. Arthur will be monstrously disappointed when he finds out that it's not true."

"So will Flora," he admitted reluctantly. "She's quite given up on me now that she realizes that I intend never to marry. Perhaps 'tis cruel of us to give her false hopes. However, perchance no connection will be made between our actions."

"I think that hardly likely when we've been the cause of so much gossip, do you?"

He grimaced. "Sadly, no. We must hope that our quest doesn't take us overlong. It would not do that we should be gone too lengthy a time. As it is, we must evolve some explanation that will prove acceptable. Without some such, it will be deemed that I've ruined you. Your reputation will be in tatters. Didn't you think of the consequences before setting out on such an expedition?"

She hung her head, scuffing her toes as they walked. "To be honest, Edward, I didn't give it any thought. My one desire was to salvage Freddie. I shouldn't have embroiled you in my schemes, but you were the only one I thought I could safely turn to."

A light of devilment lit his eyes. "What of Melville? Would he not have served your cause equally well?"

Stopping in her tracks, she cast him a disparaging look, one almost of disgust. "Edward Thurston, you are hateful. Why do you find it necessary to be always throwing Melville at my head?"

"I thought you favored him," he said innocently.

"I most certainly do not!"

"Then whom do you favor?"

"I favor no one!" she replied hotly. "And should you find it necessary to pursue this train of thought, I will continue this journey on my own. I will not be cross-examined on the subject."

"Caught a raw nerve, have I, Jen?"

"No!" she cried, increasing her pace and going before him.

Sinclair followed, watching with amusement the straightening of her shoulders and the effort she put into her step. However, he was loath for any discord to exist between them, and, lengthening his stride, he caught up with her. Jenny cast him a sidelong glance beneath her lashes but forbore any comment, and within minutes an easy camaraderie existed once more.

It was fully dark by the time they finally arrived at their destination, the sign above the doorway proclaiming that they'd reached The King's Arms.

When they entered the small inn, muted sounds came from the taproom set to the left. Opening the door sufficiently to seek out the landlord, Sinclair was pleased to note that there appeared no more than a few locals taking their ease. The landlord came forward, a look akin to astonishment on his round, cheerful face. Never before had members of The Quality patronized his humble establishment, and it took him quite by surprise to find such visitors in his hallway. For, as he said in a hasty aside to his wife, who'd just appeared from the kitchen at the rear, these were no ordinary travelers. It confounded him to find them afoot and with no visible means of transport. Even the earl's explanation of the accident in the lane didn't satisfy his curiosity, and he wondered why someone who was obviously of the gentry should be traveling on the common coach. Nonetheless, he was more than willing to offer them the hospitality of his modest establishment.

Standing in the low-pitched entrance hall, Sinclair made known his requirements. "I would be grateful if you would provide a room for myself and another for my pupil," he said.

The landlord appeared much disconcerted. "We've . . . we've but one bedchamber that would be suitable, sir. The others would not do you—not at all. Could not the boy share it with you?"

"Definitely not," replied the earl. Then, as some explanation was obviously necessary, he added, "He snores!"

Jennifer turned sharply toward her traveling companion, casting him a look of extreme indignation, and she was even more angered to encounter the look of amusement in his eyes.

"I am quite in sympathy with you, sir," replied the landlord. "Perhaps it would prove beneficial to you if the young gentleman had a truckle bed set up in the closet?"

"As the hour is late and there appears no alternative, it would seem that arrangement will have to suffice," replied the earl, taking hold of Jennifer's elbow and giving it a meaningful squeeze to prevent any thoughts of rebellion. "Do you have a parlor?"

"Yes, sir."

"Then I would be obliged if you would waste no time in serving us supper there."

The landlord bowed them into a small cozy room at the rear of the house that was obviously intended for his own family's use but had hastily been vacated in honor of the newly arrived visitors.

"Would a supper of ham and eggs with a veal pie suit you, your honor?" he asked. "And perhaps a nice slice of apple pie? My wife's very well known for her apple pie."

"It would suit admirably," replied Sinclair, not at all daunted by the prospect of such plain fare. "Ale too, and lemonade for the la—lad."

"You were going to say *lady,* weren't you?" accused Jennifer as the landlord withdrew and they made themselves comfortable in the two winged chairs set before the hearth. "I might have known you wouldn't be able to keep up the masquerade."

"You caught me out." The earl laughed. "Even after I'd been so careful as to ensure that we had separate rooms."

"I will not qualify that remark with a reply," returned Jennifer haughtily.

Sinclair's eyes sparkled with mirth. "Have no fear, it is I who will sleep in the closet, *Jem,* and you will be assured of your comfort."

Jennifer remained indignant, despite not being entirely impervious to the gleam in her companion's eye. "Couldn't you have thought of some excuse other than I snore? I'm sure that if it had been the other way about, I could've found a more noble explanation."

"Then perhaps I am not as practiced at bending the truth as you would appear to be, Jeremiah."

An extremely incensed response was prevented at that moment by the arrival of the ham and eggs and veal pie. Neither had been aware of just how hungry they'd become, and, seating themselves at the small table, they set to with great zeal.

"Country air certainly improves one's appetite," commented Jennifer as they awaited the appearance of the apple pie.

"At least I need have no fear of you wasting away, my dear," commented the earl with some amusement. "It's quite refreshing to see a young lady who doesn't find it necessary to declare she has the appetite of a bird. I fail to see the sense in that."

"Then you've not been schooled in the niceties of a young lady in society. One must appear to scarcely need sustenance, to preserve one's ethereal air. Besides, you said that I must behave as a scrubby schoolboy. I merely do as I am bid."

"A role you fill quite admirably. One would suspect you born to it." He laughed, unable to contain his amusement further. "I can scarcely believe you to be the same elegant Lady Jennifer who is the darling of society. You've taken on a surprising new persona—one I never would have suspected you capable of, although one I must admit to having taken a liking to."

The apple pie arrived fresh from the oven, the landlady bringing a jug of thick cream that she thought the young gentleman would like, and she patted Jen's cheek as she passed. "You remind me so of my youngest boy," she commented. Encountering a strange look from the earl, she dropped a hasty curtsy. "Begging the sir's pardon, I'm sure," she said, making a hurried exit.

It was as well that she did not stay, for she would've thought it most strange to see the two gentlemen engaged in a most unseemly bout of laughter.

The closet, connected to the small but neat bedchamber by a door, proved to be no more than a cupboard. The truckle bed almost filled its entire space, making it difficult for the earl to stand inside. He had to bend his head to enter, his broad shoulders almost filling the doorway. Jennifer laughed at his predicament as she sat hugging her knees on the large bed.

"I do think we would fare much better if I slept in there." She giggled, watching his efforts to ease his frame into the small space allowed. "I don't need half the room that you do. I could be quite comfortable."

Grinning ruefully, the earl stepped reluctantly back into the bedroom. "I doubt the bed would take my length, though it would be less than noble of me to consign you to such a fate."

"Nonsense!" she cried, coming to her feet. "I would be quite cozy in there." Pushing past him, she sat on the bed. "See? I fit perfectly."

Seeing the sense of the arrangement, Sinclair could do naught but agree, though he liked not the thought that she was forced to endure the cramped conditions of the closet. "You must leave the door ajar, should you have need of me," he ordered. "And if you become uncomfortable, we must exchange places."

"Stop wittering, Edward," she admonished, smiling impishly up at him. "I will do extremely well in here if you would just pass my bag so that I may undress."

He passed her bag, and the door was closed while she prepared to retire.

Taking up his own valise, he laid it on the bed and opened the straps, but, as he put his hand inside, his fingers encountered a small oval object, and he lifted it from its resting place. Even in the dim light cast by the lone candle, he knew what he held. It was the portrait. Hastily he pushed it back into the valise; it would not do that his companion should see it. He could not believe that he'd been so foolish as to bring it with him, but so used had he become to having it always with him that, in his inebriated state, he must have automatically packed it along with his other necessities.

Seeing that the closet door remained closed, he retrieved the miniature once more. Taking it to the window, he drew the curtain slightly to one side so that the moon's pale light shone weakly on the sweet face. His lips slowly curved into a smile as his eyes caressed each feature, his senses drinking in her fragile beauty. He studied it for as long as he dared before raising it to his lips and then once more replacing it among his belongings, knowing that Jennifer must never see it.

Chapter Five

When they arrived in the parlor in pursuit of breakfast the following morning, the landlord waited on them immediately. Being the only travelers at the inn, they received his undivided attention. "Did you sleep well in the closet, young sir?" he asked as he brought Jennifer a cup of tea and deposited coffee before the earl.

"Quite cozily, thank you," she replied with some amusement, sobering slightly at a warning glance from her companion but unable to resist temptation. "Though I must tell you, I am not the only one who may be accused of snoring."

"Touché, Jeremiah." The earl grinned as the landlord left the room chuckling. "*Do* I snore, *Jem*?"

"I wouldn't know, *Ned*," she replied mischievously, waiting for the rebuff, but none came. "I must have fallen asleep long before you." Then after a moment's silence she asked, "May I call you Ned? It has such a comfortable feel to it."

Sinclair grinned. "You may call me what you will, my dear. Indeed, if we are to continue on such a footing, I think it would be advisable. Perhaps at our next encounter you might like to introduce me as your brother. It will make our association less formal and enable you to take the name of Thurston rather than Scatterwell, with which you have been so ignobly christened."

"Do I have to remain Jeremiah?" she asked hopefully. "Couldn't another name be found?"

"Jem it must remain, I'm afraid. It would not do to risk a slip and raise curiosity."

"Then let it be Jeremy, should the need arise. It's *slightly* more noble."

"Very well. Jeremy Thurston you shall become. Welcome to the family, my dear."

She gave him a curious look, to which he raised an inquiring brow.

"What now, Jem? Why so suddenly serious?"

"It's so like the name I very nearly had—Jenny Thurston."

He rose abruptly from the table, almost upsetting his coffee in the process. "We cannot go back to those times, Jenny," he said in a hardened voice. "I gave you my reasons, and they remain. You will thank me soon enough."

"I, too, certainly have no wish to resume our engagement," she replied with equal coldness. "Though not for the same reasons as you, I suspect."

"Then what are your reasons, Jenny? Tell me now, and have done with it. Whatever they are, you will find no opposition. Indeed, in all probability I will agree with you. Therefore, speak; I am prepared for the worst."

For a moment she regarded him rebelliously, before replying in a defiant tone, "My reasons are, Edward Thurston, that you gave me no opportunity to get to know you. I am well aware that you proposed to me at the instigation of our families. Your offer was made merely out of a sense of obligation. . . ."

"You had no objection at the time," he interjected harshly. "If I remember correctly, you appeared to almost welcome the match."

"I was young. I didn't realize the implications. Almost immediately you were posted to Spain, and when I attempted to get to know you through your letters, all you ever mentioned were trivialities. How could I marry a man who had no desire to know me? I would as soon remain unwed than to enter into such a marriage."

"Very succinctly put, my dear. You echo my sentiments exactly. Though I would make just a small addition to that statement. I would also prefer to remain unwed than contract a marriage where my wife is compelled to view me with either revulsion or pity."

Instantly she was on her feet and would have given a hasty reply, but at that moment the landlady bustled into the parlor bearing a hearty breakfast, which she laid on the table before bobbing a brief curtsy and once more retreating to the kitchen.

For several heartbeats they stood looking defiantly at each other, both unwilling to make the first move until, relenting, the earl said in rallying tones, "What, not hungry, Jem? We may spend all morning quarrelling like children if you so desire, but I must admit, I would welcome my breakfast."

Reluctantly she resumed her seat, watching from beneath lowered lashes as the earl did the same. There were still words she would have said, but instead she had to content herself by muttering, "You are hateful, Edward, and I wish I had not invited you on this journey."

"An invite, was it, my girl?" He chuckled, with eyebrows raised, his humor returned. "I was of the opinion that when you presented yourself at my house, it was more of a royal command."

"I did do it rather well, didn't I?" she replied, her eyes sparkling with merriment. "I knew you would find it difficult to refuse me, though you almost ruined it all by coming home foxed."

"I realize my intoxication must have proved a severe trial to you, brat. Though, the next time you have need of my services, I would appreciate a little more notice."

"Then you truly don't regret coming with me?" she asked in a hopeful voice.

"I truly do not."

Content with his reply, she settled to her meal, and a feeling of rapport existed between them once more.

Once the meal was over, neither felt the inclination to continue with their previous discussion, feeling that the topic had been exhausted and the air cleared.

"I've been thinking," said the earl, pushing away his plate. "Instead of trying to rejoin the stage, I believe we may now safely travel post. We are far enough away from London for it not to make any difference. What say you? Have you had your fill of public conveyances?"

"I rather enjoyed the experience." Jennifer chuckled. "We met such interesting company. Indeed, it was extremely diverting."

"I never knew you were such a chatterbox." He grinned. "You talked incessantly and with scarcely any caution. Forswear, I was in constant fear of our being found out, although you certainly seemed to relish your role of schoolboy. However, I think it advisable that we recommence our journey in more comfort. Without it being necessary to pick up and deposit passengers, we should reach Freddie that much sooner."

"Couldn't we delay our journey just a little, Ned?" she said unexpectedly. "This is such a cozy inn, and it wouldn't do Freddie any harm to reflect on his misdeeds. Forswear, it may even do him some good."

"Let him stew, you mean? I can see the sense in that, but it would not do that we tarry. We cannot spend another night under this roof. Think of the impropriety of the situation and the scandal we would cause should our whereabouts become known."

"Who's to know where we are? It isn't a route frequented by society, and the inn is so small, it could easily pass unnoticed. It's so pleasant here. Couldn't we stay just one more night? I promise I will not plague you. *Please,* Ned."

Sinclair found it difficult to resist the pleading in her voice but, realizing he must stand firm, curtly replied, "No. We must make what speed we can so we can resolve the situation as soon as possible. Go and prepare for the journey. I will ask the landlord for directions to the nearest posting inn."

It was not until Jennifer rejoined the earl in the parlor a short while later that he had the opportunity to discuss the matter with the landlord.

"The Red Fox is the inn you want, sir," said the proprietor. "You'll have no difficulty in hiring a chaise there, though it's a tidy step away from here."

"And how far is a 'tidy step'?" inquired Sinclair.

"I should say about seven miles, as the crow flies."

"It's a lovely day. We could easily walk there," enthused Jennifer.

"My dear Jem, you are not a bird, and neither am I," was the earl's dampening reply. "Although I have every confidence in your ability to walk seven miles, I don't think it wise to attempt it."

"I have a gig that you could drive over to the Red Fox," said the landlord, eager to be of some assistance. "Our eldest son works at the smithy, and he could return it to me when he finishes for the day."

"Does he walk the seven miles to work?" asked Jennifer, curious.

"He does, young sir, so he will be glad of the ride home."

"If your son is able to walk that distance before a day's work, I am quite sure that we could. . . ."

"No, we could not!" interposed Sinclair with some force. Turning to the landlord, he said, "We will take the gig and thank you for it."

"I will put the horse to the shafts immediately, sir," said the landlord. "He's young but a sweet-enough goer."

The post chaise bowled out of the yard at the Red Fox, its occupants appreciating its comparative comforts to their previous mode of travel.

"I must admit, post has definite advantages over the common coach," confided Jennifer.

"I thought you'd found it quite amusing." The earl chuckled, sitting opposite his companion, easing his long legs out before him, and crossing his ankles. "Now, alas, you have only me to entertain you."

"Sadly, 'tis a circumstance I will have to bear with what fortitude I can muster," said Jennifer, smiling in return, longing to emulate his position but realizing it would appear most unladylike.

"As we are traveling post, I've decided that we can now forgo the dubious pleasures of Coventry and take a more direct route to our destination. Therefore, we need spend only one further night en route."

"Where will that be?"

"I know of a posting house in Oakham—not intimately but by repute. It's said to offer excellent accommodation and a more than adequate bill of fare."

She appeared to consider this. "But if it's been recommended, will it not also be know to other members of the ton? And who knows who might be patronizing it? Perhaps a lesser-known inn would suffice."

"I think you might have the right of it, Jen," replied the earl thoughtfully. "I will ask the coachman if he can recommend an establishment. I wouldn't wish to prolong our journey."

"You will be glad to be rid of me?"

"Of the situation—of course. The thought of the torment young Freddie must be suffering is intolerable."

"I would almost say he deserves it," said Jennifer tartly. "He should have more sense than to enter into a bout of fisticuffs."

"Sometimes such situations are unavoidable," replied Sinclair. "He may have had no alternative but to defend himself. Tempers flare more quickly than reason."

"I can't imagine *you* being led into such a situation."

Sinclair laughed. "Do I appear so sensible? For I assure you, I am not."

"You are known to be very tolerant, Ned."

"If I'm to be accused of tolerance now, it's merely because I remember like instances in my youth when I was equally as hotheaded as our respective brothers. Perhaps even more so, until entering the cavalry moderated my moods."

"I don't believe it for one minute. Arthur told me you were ever known for your even temper."

"You would wish me otherwise?" he asked with some surprise. "If I was, I would not have attempted this journey. I would have returned you home immediately."

"Edward Thurston . . ." she began.

He laughed. "I know, I know—'Edward Thurston, I hate you.' "

"I was about to say," replied Jennifer, feigning superiority, "that I don't believe you for one moment. You are far more generous than that, and you certainly don't appear averse to the situation. Indeed, one could almost accuse you of enjoying the experience."

"That's as may be, my girl," he said, finally relenting. "You seem to have the measure of me. Though what Flora would say if she could see us, I know not. She's confirmed that I've become very staid and dull. If she could see me cavorting about the countryside with a hoyden of a girl masquerading first as my pupil and now as my brother, I doubt she would be of the same opinion."

"Arthur would be only too thankful to be rid of me; indeed, he's often told me so."

The earl's dark brows snapped into a frown. "You're not welcome in your own home?" he asked with great concern.

"I am decidedly *de trop*. He wishes to marry and for he and his wife to be the sole occupants of the house."

"What of you and Freddie?"

"He cares not what becomes of us. He daren't coerce me into marriage, though frequently his methods come near to it."

"Your life is made uncomfortable?" Sinclair asked, concern heavy in his voice.

"At times."

"Damn him," he swore forcefully. "Am I to suppose that when our engagement was broken, he was less than charitable to you?"

"Considerably so. He saw his own plans thwarted and re-acted accordingly."

For quite a few moments he said nothing, the heavy frown remaining on his brow as he stared sightlessly through the window. Eventually he returned his gaze to his companion, and, sitting forward in his seat, he reached out and took her hand.

"You must forgive me, Jenny," he said earnestly. "It was not my intention to put you into an invidious position."

At the touch of his fingers, she hastily withdrew her hand. "There's no need to apologize," she said quickly. "I was of the same frame of mind as you. I must take my share of the blame. Indeed, I'd already informed Arthur of my intention of ending the betrothal before I came to see you at Fly."

"Then it came as no great shock to you when I followed the same course?" he asked, watching from beneath lowered brows as he once more sat back in his seat.

"It rankled that you were the first to state the case. As is common in these situations, I would have preferred to be the one to make the break. I'd come to Fly with the intention of explaining all to you."

"And I was too eager to say my piece," he stated flatly.

"You did seem somewhat eager to be rid of the betrothal—and me—yes."

"I wished only to assure you that you were in no way obli-gated to proceed with the marriage, that we would not deal at all well together. I put my case too bluntly, but I had no wish to wound you."

She considered the matter briefly, studying his face. "We do well enough as friends though, don't we, Ned?"

"Aye, as friends we do admirably." He smiled, and then a teasing light came into his eyes. "Though I could wish for a lit-tle more respect from my young brother when in company. I will not have it announced to all and sundry that I snore when it was you who kept me awake half the night with your mutterings."

She picked up her hat from the seat beside her and, laughing, threw it at his head, but he deftly caught it before it made contact.

"I said you were a hoyden." He laughed, placing the hat out of her reach. "Heaven help the man who finally takes you to wife. He does so with my deepest sympathy."

"That need not worry you, Edward," she replied haughtily. "It's no concern of yours. I, too, have decided never to marry."

"Then that is a great pity, my dear."

She moved to a corner of the coach and sat with chin resting in hand as she studied the passing countryside, and silence reigned.

"I've spoken to the coachman, and he suggests either The Pheasant or an inn that has the dubious name of The Sow's Ear," the earl informed Jennifer when next they stopped to change horses and alighted to partake of refreshment. "He informs me that The Pheasant is often frequented by sporting gentlemen on their way to the races, so 'twould appear that The Sow's Ear may be more suitable. What say you, Jem? Do you think you could be comfortable in an inn that rejoices in such a name?"

"If it's the quieter of the two, then most certainly," replied Jennifer, finishing the last of her cold lamb. "If we wish to remain undiscovered, it appears we've no choice in the matter. 'Pon reflection, 'tis quite a colorful name."

"Then we must hope the patrons to be less so and that we are able to secure separate bedchambers. It would not do to tempt providence a second time and risk discovery."

Sinclair drained the last of his ale and rose from the table, indicating that she should do the same, and, after paying the shot, he guided her once more to the waiting chaise.

Once inside and the journey resumed, he said, "I've been thinking, Jenny. Tomorrow I believe it would be prudent to break our journey at Ashbourne and for you to change into your skirts. It won't do that you should arrive at our destination in your guise of schoolboy. It would only complicate matters."

"What of the coachman and postillion—will they not think

it strange?" she asked in some surprise. She'd not given her new persona a second thought or even contemplated her reception when she should at last confront Freddie.

"From the curious stare the coachman gave you at our last halt, I believe he may have his suspicions already," the earl informed her. "He may even believe he's party to an elopement."

"Pish, who would elope to Buxton?" she scoffed. "If we'd been bound for the border, then I could understand his reasoning. But Buxton? No!"

"You have brought a suitable gown with you, haven't you?"

"Of course I have," she replied indignantly.

"Then I will have no argument. You will change into it tomorrow."

She firmed her chin, casting him a mutinous look. "What if I refuse?"

"That would not be wise," he said severely. "You will not refuse. We make a stop at Ashbourne."

"And if I don't comply?" she persisted.

"Then I will find it necessary to dress you myself."

"You wouldn't dare."

"There you have the wrong of it, my dear. I most certainly would dare."

"Edward!" came her incensed reply. "I would not have believed it of you!"

He laughed. "That shows just how little you know me, Jeremiah. If you challenge me, I will most certainly carry out my threat."

"Edward Thurston . . ."

"I know. I know," he said, laughing. "I've heard it often enough."

"Well, I do. I hate you!"

It lacked but five minutes to ten when the travelers laid weary foot in the small, dimly lit private parlor of The Sow's Ear. A general hum emanated from the taproom on the other side of the corridor, but other than that, the inn appeared sparsely inhabited. To the earl's relief, two bedchambers were secured, albeit on different floors. Ordering their supper to be served as soon as possible, they determined that once the meal was over, they would immediately seek repose.

"The young gentleman looks quite done up, sir," confided the proprietor to the earl when he ordered the repast.

Jennifer cast him a tired glance as she took her seat on the settle beside the small fire that made the room less chilly. She had been quiet for some time and felt disinclined to enter into conversation, leaving Sinclair to make what arrangements were necessary.

"I trust I chose rightly for supper?" asked the earl, taking his seat on the opposite side of the hearth.

She nodded briefly, even this seeming an effort in her weary state.

"Try not to fall asleep, my dear," said Sinclair softly, as he watched her eyelids begin to fall. "You will only feel the worse for it."

"I am not going to sleep. I merely rest my eyes," lied Jenny valiantly, as her head drooped onto her chest.

Rising from his seat, the earl gently lifted her feet from the floor so that she lay on the settle. He attempted to ease her into a more comfortable position, cursing softly at what he perceived as his clumsiness, with having but one arm to achieve the task. However, she nestled quite contentedly on the ill-padded seat, murmuring slightly as she rested her head in the crook of her arm. He tried to catch her words, but they were inaudible, and he resumed his seat.

He sat studying his companion's sleeping countenance. As he took in her sleep-softened features and tousled hair, his own expression softened in contemplation, but the moment of reverie was short-lived as the maids arrived with the meal. He raised his hand to indicate that they should go quietly about their task, but their clattering as they laid the meal on the table roused Jenny, and she slowly raised herself up.

"I was not asleep, Ned," she mumbled, rubbing her eyes. "I promise you, I was not asleep."

"Of course you weren't." He smiled indulgently. "You merely rested your eyes. I know you are tired, but try to take some nourishment, and then you may seek your bed."

"I'm too tired. Couldn't I just sleep? You can wake me when you've finished."

Taking her arm, he raised her from the settle, slowly pulling her to her feet. "Even if it's only the broth, you must take something, Jen. Come, sit at the table, and you will feel more awake."

With lagging steps, she did as he bade her, taking the chair he held for her. "Am I a trial to you, Ned?" she asked with a wan smile.

"A severe trial, my dear," he said, a wealth of warmth in his eyes and voice as, taking his own seat, he pushed the broth toward her. "Though I must tell you that at this precise moment you bear a distinct resemblance to a dormouse."

She chuckled drowsily. "I quite like dormice."

"So do I, my dear, so do I," he said soberly, and, pressing the spoon into her hand, he bade her eat.

They spoke little during the meal; it was not necessary, so comfortable were they in each other's company. Once the meal was over, the earl pushed his chair from the table and, standing, placed his arm about Jennifer and raised her to her feet.

"Come, I will assist you to your bedchamber," he said softly. "We leave at first light so that we may complete our journey. You will feel more revived in the morning."

She laid her head against his shoulder, allowed him to lead her from the room, and with his aid mounted the stairs to the first landing. As they achieved the corridor, a figure started out of the shadows and, pushing past them, quickly descended the stairs to disappear into the taproom.

"Who was that?" asked Jenny, lifting her head from his shoulder to look in the direction of the vanishing figure.

"Probably one of the locals," replied the earl, frowning slightly. But there had been nothing of the local about the cut of the man's garb. Indeed, in the poor light there appeared something familiar about his shadowed countenance, but he would not tell Jenny. He had no wish to alarm her.

Closing the bedchamber door softly as he left his sleepy charge with instructions to lock it after him, Sinclair, instead of seeking his own repose, once more descended to the ground floor. He stood for a moment outside the taproom door before pushing it wide. Due to the lateness of the hour, the dimly lit room was almost deserted. Only a few hardy individuals remained to sit over their ale. He scanned their faces as each looked toward the door to see who entered, but none seemed familiar. Taking one last look, he decided that he must have been mistaken in thinking he knew the man on the stair, and, returning to the parlor, he ordered a bottle of brandy to be brought to him.

The hour was quite advanced before the earl forsook the parlor and, taking a candle from the hallway, once more climbed the stairs to his own bedchamber. Entering the darkened room, he placed the candle on the small table beside the bed and, in its flickering light, prepared to retire.

Taking the portrait from the valise, he climbed between the sheets. Lying back against the pillows, by the candle's soft light, he examined the beauty's features, his mind taking a fanciful turn. However, his tender musings were brought to an abrupt end when he heard a soft footfall pause outside his door and saw the light of a candle halt there. Pushing the miniature hastily beneath the pillows, he watched as a shadow appeared to move tentatively in the corridor, and the thought of the man on the stair once more crossed his mind. He'd been unable to identify the half-hidden features, but it left him with a feeling of unease.

He pushed aside the covers and, leaving the bed, stepped quietly to the door, seeing the handle move noiselessly. Immediately he reached for his breeches, which lay on a hard chair by the hearth, and, pulling them on as best he could, he sprung wide the door. The hallway appeared empty, only shadows inhabiting the poorly lit corridor. Hearing a door close in the darkness, he reasoned that it must have been a like visitor who, in the ill light, had mistaken his door for his own. Trying the latch but finding a resistance there, his fellow guest must have realized that he mistook the door and in so doing had found his own.

Berating himself for having allowed his imagination to over-rule reason, he once more returned to his bed, extinguishing his candle and seeking repose.

It was barely dawn when a tapping on his door woke him and Jenny quietly but insistently called his name. When he gave a mumbled reply, her voice became more imperative in tone.

"Let me in, Ned. Please let me in."

"What is it?" he asked, quickly leaving his bed and reaching for his breeches, cursing himself for his clumsiness as he hastily dragged them on.

"Just let me in," she pleaded urgently, and, without thinking, he reached and turned the key in the lock.

Immediately she pushed open the door and came into the room, closing it noiselessly behind her. She came to an abrupt halt. Observing him in the half light, she momentarily froze, seeing for the first time the scarring to his upper body.

He heard her sharp intake of breath and desperately tried to pull on his shirt, but in his haste he fumbled, and it fell to the floor. Immediately she was before him, eager to assist.

"Leave it alone," he demanded in an awful voice. "Leave me. I don't need your help. I'm no puling infant."

"Ned, I . . ." she began, a catch in her voice, but he pushed her roughly aside.

"Turn your back. I will not have your eyes on me," he commanded, desperate that she should not see his injuries.

She did as he bid, but he could see her shoulders shaking as she gave vent to tears.

Full of remorse, he roughly pulled the shirt over his head and forced his arm into the sleeve.

For a moment he hesitated. He regretted his actions, but it affected him so that she should see his disfigurement. As her distress became more apparent, he went to her, putting his arm about her shoulders.

"Come, sweeting," he cajoled, drawing her to his side. "I do not wish to wound you, but you must not see me like this."

She turned to him and buried her face against his chest, clutching at the ill-used shirt.

"I was frightened. . . ." she offered in explanation, tears still sounding in her voice.

"Of me?" he asked sharply. "Am I so hideous?"

"Oh, no, Ned, no," she cried. "Never that. Someone came to my door a few moments ago and tried the lock. I thought it was you and called your name, but whoever it was laughed softly—horribly—and left. It terrified me, and I needed you."

He held her tightly to him to comfort her, and she heard the steady thud of his heart and felt the comforting strength of his embrace, and her fears calmed.

"My lock was also tried in the early hours," he said, frowning. "I know not who it might be or what their intentions, but I believe we should leave immediately. If there are thieves abroad, we won't present them with opportunity. Remain here while I finish dressing, and then together we will go to your room to collect your bag. I will order the coachman to put to immediately."

Perched on the ladder-back chair, Jenny waited while Sinclair completed his dressing. Perceiving the difficulty he had in carrying out this task, she would have gone instantly to his aid, but she knew he would not welcome her intervention. Indeed, she knew that any offer of assistance would only result in rejection.

As the coach drew away from the inn, Jennifer was conscious that a certain reserve remained in the earl's manner and was only too aware of its origins. He made no attempt at conversation. Instead, he turned slightly away from her, as if studying the passing countryside.

They traveled some miles in silence before, unable to stand the discord any longer, she forsook her seat to sit at Sinclair's side. He turned his head briefly, giving but a slight smile in recognition before continuing his contemplation of the passing scenery. His dark brows were drawn into a heavy frown, and his face appeared pale in the morning light, and her heart went out to him.

Hesitantly she slipped her hand into his elbow in an attempt to gain his attention, but he resisted the temptation to turn toward her.

Unwilling to let the matter rest, she said in a small voice, "We've never spoken of your injuries, Ned."

"Nor shall we. There's no need," he replied in a harsh voice. "My disfigurement is plain for all to see. It will not improve with discussion."

"You wrong me if you think I see it as a disfigurement," she said earnestly, tightening her hold on his arm. "I see not the injury but the man. You've no wish for pity, and I do not offer it. You are as strong and vital as you ever were, and that is how you are perceived. You are no object for sympathy."

He gave no answer, but she saw that the tension about his lips relaxed slightly and the thunder seeped from his brow. Eventually he turned toward her. "You must forgive me, Jenny," he said softly, taking her hand. "I've so long feared what would be the reaction to the ravages wreaked on my frame. I am no longer the man you once thought me, and it's abhorrent to me to evoke either fear or pity."

"I don't see you as a candidate for either," she said, her fingers tightening on his. "Indeed, you are no less a man than you ever were. The loss of your arm is nothing to me; I see only your goodness and vigor and—"

Suddenly the coachman rapped on the roof. "We are nearing Ashbourne, sir," he announced as the earl opened the hatch.

"Then we will make a stop before continuing to Buxton," replied Sinclair, thankful for a diversion from the intensity of their conversation. He found it a conversation hard to pursue, deciding it would serve no purpose to examine their separate emotions too closely. Aware that his own lay too near the surface, he feared that in an unguarded moment he would find them too difficult to suppress.

Returning his attention to his companion, he said, "As soon as we arrive at the inn, I will arrange for a bedchamber to be put at your disposal."

"You still wish me to change?" said Jenny, her chin firming.

The earl grinned ruefully, his eyes lighting with amusement. "As delighted as I've been to see you in schoolboy garb, my dear, for the sake of your reputation I do believe it is necessary for your metamorphosis into a young lady once more."

"Must I, Ned? Is it really necessary?"

"Imperative, Jen. Your entry into Buxton will be as a young lady of quality."

In answer she once more removed herself to the seat opposite, folding her arms defiantly across her chest.

"Why the long face?" queried the earl. "Freddie is within your reach, and all will be put to rights."

"It means the end of our adventure, Ned."

" 'Adventure'? Is that what you would call it?" He laughed. "You will find it less of an adventure when we are forced to face the comments upon our return."

"I'd quite forgotten about that," she said, sitting upright in her seat. "Do you think it will be very bad?"

"Undoubtedly," was his only reply.

Chapter Six

Once installed in a bedchamber at the posting inn, Jennifer cast aside her jacket and breeches and lifted the pale blue dimity dress from the bed. At any other time she would have been quite happy to wear it, deeming it most suitable as a day dress to be worn in the country. However, today it found no favor with her, and it was with a reluctant sigh that she stepped into it and arranged a white lace fichu about her shoulders.

Taking a hand mirror from the cloak bag, she attempted to brush her shorn curls into a more feminine style, which only served to make her look even more elfin. She had not thought of the consequences when she'd taken the scissors and cut her beautiful dark locks so short; it had not occurred to her that she would appear most strange when going about in society. However, now that she was not obliged to brush those locks severely back from her brow to fit her boyish role, she could see that the style became her, and she smiled at the thought of what the tabbies would say of it.

"Now we will see what *you* make of me, Edward Thurston,"

she whispered to her reflection before placing the mirror once more into the bag.

"There, do I now have your approval?" she asked, stepping into the inn's wainscoted private parlor and executing a neat little curtsy before the earl.

Sinclair rose from a chair by the hearth and made a profound leg. "Lady Jennifer—Jenny." He smiled, coming forward. "It would now seem that I must treat you with the respect due your station." Taking the hand she proffered in salute, he raised it dutifully to his lips. "My dear, the transformation is complete. You look enchanting, though how we will explain the shortness of your hair, I know not."

"Do I look a fright?" she asked anxiously, her hand going automatically to her curls.

"Not at all, Jen." He chuckled. "A little unconventional, but a delight, I assure you. Within a week you will have society paying homage and emulating your daring new look. I will lay odds on it."

"Does it find favor with *you,* Ned?" she asked, watching his reaction from beneath lowered lashes.

Smiling, he tweaked her curls. "Have I not said so? But I will not feed your vanity. It's not, after all, with me that you need find favor but with the many beaux who prostrate themselves at your feet."

This was not at all the reply she'd been looking for, and it drove her to retort haughtily, "I wish I could reply in kind, Edward, but you seem to show not the slightest interest in attaching any young lady's affections."

"I've no time for petticoats," he mocked, retreating to the settle once more. "I am quite content with my lot."

"You, sir, are a misogynist," she snapped, stamping her foot.

"There you have the wrong of it, Jenny." He laughed. "*Quite* the wrong of it."

Congratulating himself on his perception of the matter, the coachman gave a knowing smile and winked meaningfully at the postillion as he assisted his passengers into the waiting equipage.

As he took up the reins to commence the final few miles to Buxton, he thought of the tale with which he would regale his wife upon his return, for he had suspected the young sir of being a girl—and a very pretty one to boot. However, he saw that the miss seemed less than pleased when she emerged from the inn, and he diagnosed a lovers' tiff. He noted that the gentleman appeared somewhat amused by the whole, and he predicted the gent's downfall, finding nothing loverlike whatsoever in his manner. A very strange matter indeed.

The coach rolled out of the inn's yard at a spanking pace. The newly hired team was fresh, and the two travelers knew that their journey would soon be at an end.

Jennifer, retaining her air of resentment, sat erect in the forward-facing corner of the coach, while the earl sat at his ease on the opposite seat. Silence reigned for the first mile or so, a silence that begged to be broken.

As his companion appeared disinclined to set up a dialogue, Sinclair made an attempt at polite conversation. "Is this your first visit to Derbyshire, Jenny?" he asked.

"No," came her short reply, as she refused to be drawn into conversation.

"Then as it is mine, perhaps you would be so obliging as to point out any places you deem of interest."

"There are none."

"The views are quite remarkable," he persisted, attempting to hide a grin, but the light in his eyes betrayed him.

"I would prefer it if you did not speak to me, Edward Thurston," said Jennifer in an indifferent voice. "For when you do, it is merely to mock me."

"Behold, a penitent man," he teased, hanging his head. "If in some inadvertent way I have offended my lady, I offer her my profound apologies."

She laughed in response. "No, you don't. You know you don't."

"Perhaps not," he replied, grinning boyishly. "But dare I mention that it brought about the desired results? You no longer scowl at me. Possibly now would be a good time for you to inform me about the hapless individual upon whom we are about to descend. You've said very little on the subject. I take it to be a school friend of Freddie's?"

"Dear me, no. Have I not explained?" she said. "How remiss of me. 'Tis Mrs. Rutledge, a friend of my mother's who lives just on the other side of Buxton with her son, Phillip. She is a widow, and Freddie and I went to stay with her when Mother died. We were made so welcome that, had it not been for Arthur's insistence that we return to London, we would have happily remained there. Freddie and Phillip became firm friends and have remained so. As no other destination presented itself, I naturally assumed Freddie to have fled there."

"And if he has not?"

"I know of no alternative. If he isn't to be found there, I'm at a loss as to where else to look." On a sudden thought she turned anxiously toward Sinclair. "You don't think he could have run away to sea do you, Ned?"

"I think it highly unlikely. If it were Perry, then it could well be a possibility, but Freddie lacks his impetuosity and possesses a more sensible turn of mind. I agree that Buxton seems the more probable choice. We shall soon know."

Derbyshire's glorious vista spread before them as they drove through Dovedale Valley and the adjoining countryside. Both in their own way regretting that the end of the journey was in sight, they each sat lost in reverie. Occasionally Jenny cast a glance at her companion, but his averted countenance told her nothing, as he appeared absorbed in their surroundings.

Eventually they descended into Buxton, and as they drove through the modest town, she pointed to a large house situated on the rise that overlooked its cobbled streets.

"Berry House," she said, as he came to sit beside her. "That is where Mrs. Rutledge—Judith—lives."

He gave it but a cursory glance before turning to face her fully. "I've been thinking," he said, "about our return to London. . . ."

She grimaced dolefully. "So have I, and I don't see how it can be achieved without causing comment."

"Then I'm sure you'll see the sense of what I'm about to suggest."

She looked at him hopefully. "Can you see a way around it, Ned? For I'm sure I cannot."

"We will leave Buxton separately. I will return to London while you and Freddie go to my sister's house and explain all to her. I am sure Flora will need little encouragement to state that the two of you have been on a visit to her the whole time. She likes nothing more than the role of conspirator. I will send Perry to you, and he can add credence to your story. I will attempt to allay rumors in London. If it's seen that I return alone, I can say that I've been on an expedition to the races. None will dare query it in my presence. Some may have their suspicions, but none can provide proof that we've been within fifty miles of each other."

"Do you think it will serve?" she asked doubtfully. "Are you sure Flora will go along with the ploy?"

"I think I can safely put your mind at rest on that score. I know my sister well enough to guess at her reaction. She will see it as a very romantic escapade and read all manner of hopes for our future into it."

"Then I will certainly put her right on that score, Ned. Though if I do, she might be reluctant to help us."

"Not Flora. She is ever hopeful of a reconciliation between us."

"What a severe trial we must be to her." Jenny chuckled. "She seems forever destined for disappointment."

The earl dropped his gaze, studying the toe of his boot. "I hate to mention it, Jen, but what of Hawley?"

"Oh, Lord, I'd forgotten about him," she groaned, raising a hand to her brow. "How am I to face him? When we set out on the journey, I gave no thought to the fact that I would have to return. Indeed, the consequences of my actions were the furthest thing from my mind. I saw only the need to find Freddie."

"Perhaps it would be appropriate for me to pay him a visit," said Sinclair, patting her hand as it rested in her lap. "I will explain all to him, and I'm sure he'll see the sense of our arrangements."

"He won't believe our story. Even though it is the truth."

"Do you think that he should also be told that you and Freddie have been visiting Flora? Will he believe that?"

"If that were the case, why would I have felt the need to abscond in the middle of the night and not make proper arrangements? No, I don't think he'll believe it."

"You don't make life easy, do you, my dear?" He chuckled, squeezing her hand. "Then it may become necessary for me to tell him all, and you must be prepared for his reaction. I will do what I can to defuse the situation."

"Ha! Arthur doesn't frighten me," she lied valiantly. "He may make things unpleasant for a while, but I can cope with his moods. I've managed thus far."

From his vantage point in the front parlor of Berry House, a pleasant, seventeenth-century manor set in formal grounds, Freddie Lynton watched the chaise approach with a great deal of trepidation. He knew not what to expect.

Over the past few days he'd fallen prey to all manner of fears and had scarcely dared leave the security of the house. Mrs. Rutledge and her son were at present engaged below stairs and were unaware of the pending visitors.

As the chaise halted at the door, Freddie stood anxiously waiting for sight of its occupants, not daring to leave his post until he knew their identity.

Seeing Sinclair step down and hand his sister from the carriage, Freddie hotfooted it to the door, flinging it wide before a startled maid could perform the service.

"Jenny!" he cried, hurrying forward across the gravel drive. "And you, sir." He took Sinclair's hand in a painful grip, a look of vast relief on his youthful countenance. "I thought you were the runners. How did you know where to find me? Have you come to inform me that I'm a murderer? For I tell you, I've been expecting it these four days or more."

He appeared to be in great agitation, and the earl laid a calming hand on his shoulder. Raising his chin slightly, he looked in the direction of the coachman and postillion, indicating that Freddie should show more caution and quell his outpourings. "Take Jenny inside while I dismiss the coachman," he said. "I will follow directly."

Freddie did as he was bid and took his sister into the sunny entrance hall of the house, where they stood awaiting the earl. Placing a comforting arm about his shoulders, Jenny covertly searched his face and was concerned to see the effects his sleepless nights had taken on his pale countenance. However, before she could make any comment, Sinclair joined them, and Freddie turned fearful eyes toward him.

"What am I to do, sir?" he cried. "I know I should have stayed to face the consequences, but my first thought was of flight."

"There's no need for all this," stated the earl calmly, eager to allay the boy's fears. "Your opponent does very well. He was no more than stunned and recovered immediately, as you would have seen if you'd not been so intent on escape. Indeed, whatever the outcome of the bout, you should have come to me, instead of haring halfway up the country."

"Then I'm not a murderer?" breathed Freddie with great relief. "I can return home?"

"Not just yet," replied Jenny, speaking for the first time. "We must take a slight detour, but I will explain all to you later. . . ."

At that moment, the door that led to below stairs opened, and Mrs. Rutledge and her son emerged and came quickly across the hallway. Briefly Sinclair looked his amazement but quickly schooled his countenance to hide his surprise.

He'd expected Phillip Rutledge to be the same age as Freddie. He had not been prepared for the handsome, blond-haired man who appeared to be his own age and who came quickly forward to embrace Jennifer warmly. Watching the joyous reunion, he knew a moment of intense disquiet before he took himself severely to task.

Mrs. Rutledge, a pleasant-faced widow in her early fifties, pushed her son aside to gather Jenny to her. "I can't tell you how prodigiously pleased we are to see you, my dear," she said, smiling warmly. "Indeed, we were on the point of sending a letter to Hawley."

"Thank goodness we arrived in time to prevent that," breathed Jenny, pulling away.

Once more stepping forward to reclaim Jenny's attention, Rutledge said, "We saw the situation immediately and thought it only right that he should be made aware of Freddie's whereabouts."

"Arthur knows nothing of the situation," Jenny confessed. "Ned and I set out in the hope of righting the matter and preventing him from finding out."

Thus far the earl's presence had gone almost unnoticed, but her outburst drew attention to him.

"And who is this who accompanies you, Jenny?" asked Phillip, turning to face the earl with a superior air.

"Judith, Phillip, allow me to introduce the Earl of Sinclair," said Jennifer, smiling at her companions.

Sinclair made a small bow. "Your servant, ma'am," he said, accepting the hand Judith extended in greeting and taking it dutifully to his lips.

Phillip stood slightly aloof, regarding the earl with a perplexed frown. "Aren't you . . . ? Weren't you and Jenny . . . ? In short, sir, are you or are you not Jenny's betrothed?"

"Not," replied Sinclair stiffly. "As you may be aware, we ended our engagement by mutual agreement. I but accompany her to retrieve Freddie."

A look almost of relief flitted across Phillip's countenance, and he came forward to warmly shake the earl's hand, the meaning of the moment's hesitation not being entirely lost on Sinclair.

"I must thank you for giving our dear Jenny your protection," said Phillip. "It's not at all seemly that she should have traveled here alone, though one would wonder at the propriety of her traveling at all without a female companion."

Liking not his air of familiar possessiveness, the earl gave a brief nod in reply.

Judith smiled and, recollecting her duties as hostess, spread her arms wide as if to gather her flock together. "Whatever am I at, leaving everyone standing in the hall?" she said. "Let us go into the parlor, and tea will be served immediately."

As everyone repaired to the parlor, Freddie took the opportunity to pull the earl aside and draw him into the shadow of the stair.

"I say, sir, I can't tell you how relieved I am," he said earnestly. "I know you will say I deserve it, but I've been in torment these last few days."

"Then you may safely put all thoughts of it out of your mind," assured Sinclair. "It was nothing but a bout of fisticuffs that resulted in an unfortunate accident—a stupid act that will have no lasting consequences. No ill will come of it. Perry was beside himself when you disappeared, but instead of coming to me with the story, he regrettably took it to your sister. Thankfully, she did come to me, but how Hawley will react, I don't know."

Freddie's face fell. "Arthur already thinks me a numbskull, and now he will have an even lower opinion of me."

Sinclair smiled, patting the boy's shoulder reassuringly. "Then we must see what can be done to salvage the situation."

Freddie appeared much relieved but sobered as a thought came to him. "There's another matter, sir," he said hesitantly, obviously embarrassed by the situation. "I didn't have sufficient funds to pay off the chaise that brought me here and had to ask Phillip to advance me the blunt. He says he will ask my brother to reimburse him to ensure that I am made aware of my folly. He knows it will make Arthur even more furious with me. I offered to repay him as soon as I received my quarterly allowance in three weeks, but he would have none of it. I know I've no right to ask, but could you . . . ? I would be so grateful, and you know I would repay you as soon as I am back in funds."

"I will square matters with Rutledge," the earl assured him, surprised that their host had taken such a hard line when Freddie was in such obvious distress. "However, it's not your money I require in return. You will repay me by giving your sister no more cause for alarm. I want your promise that if you ever again find yourself in a like situation, you will come to me."

Freddie, suppressing the urge to throw his arms about his benefactor, merely grinned and, reaching for Sinclair's hand, grasped it firmly in both of his. "By the saints, I wish you were my brother, sir. You are always so understanding of the situations we chaps find ourselves in."

"You will find me less than understanding if you and my addle-brained brother don't moderate your ways," admonished Sinclair.

When they rejoined the others, the earl noted that Phillip and Jenny appeared engrossed in a cozy tête-à-tête, and he was aware of the smiles his former fiancée bestowed on her companion. Judith attempted to draw him into conversation, but he gave only half a mind to what she was saying until he saw her looking at him with a raised eyebrow, as if she was awaiting a suitable answer to a question.

"I do beg your pardon, Mrs. Rutledge," he said, smiling. "I'm afraid that for a brief moment my thoughts were elsewhere."

Casting a glance in the direction of her son and his companion, Judith gave a knowing smile and repeated her previous question. "They would make a handsome couple, don't you think, my lord?"

"Of a certainty," replied the earl, thankful that she couldn't read his thoughts.

"It was Jenny's mother's most fervent wish that they should make a match of it, but when she died, the child's father took it into his head to find her a more suitable husband."

"In the form of myself!"

"It would seem so. Though now that the engagement is at an end, perhaps Hawley could be persuaded to look kindly on the match. They deal prodigiously well together, as you can see."

"They do indeed," agreed Sinclair pensively. Then, after a moment's pause, he said, "I would say they deal *extremely* well together."

"I knew you would see it," enthused Mrs. Rutledge. " 'Tis plain for all to see. If only Jenny would acknowledge it."

"She has reservations?"

"The child states she thinks of Phillip only as a brother, though, seeing them together, one would question it. What think you, sir?"

The earl considered the pair before giving his answer. "It's not for me to say, madam. I'm not privy to Jenny's thoughts."

" 'Madam'?" Mrs. Rutledge chuckled. "I will not have you stand on such ceremony. You must call me Judith, as do Freddie and Jenny."

Sinclair smiled, bowing slightly in his seat. "Then Judith it will be, and you, in turn, must address me as Edward. I am not overly fond of titles either."

"Freddie told us what a top-rate fellow he thought you"— she smiled—"and, in confidence, I must tell you just how disappointed he is that you are not to be his brother-in-law."

The earl studied Freddie, who had joined his sister. "He's very much akin to my own brother, and the door to my home is ever open to him, though I've no wish to encroach upon his relationship with Hawley."

"From what the boy says, he stands somewhat in awe of his brother, and when I told him that Phillip was intent on sending a letter, he was most distressed. Indeed, I can't help but regret Phillip's haste in the matter."

"I agree. Without it, we might have a chance to salvage the situation, as was our intention. But if Hawley had been informed, we would have had little chance of achieving it. However, I am hoping that with my sister, Flora's, assistance, we may yet be able to avoid a scandal. We left London in some haste, none being aware of our whereabouts, and it will take a good deal of ingenuity to bring about a satisfactory conclusion to the matter."

"You are rather flouting propriety, you know, accompanying Jenny without as much as a maid for chaperone," said Judith.

"Forswear, if the nature of your journey should become known, she will be ruined, and you would be obliged to marry her, whether it's what you both wish or not."

"Even though we are no longer betrothed, you must know that I would go to any lengths to preserve her reputation," Sinclair assured her.

"I do believe you would," said Judith, considering the point. "I see that Freddie did not exaggerate when he stated his opinion of you, and I can understand his regret that the engagement was broken."

The earl smiled, appearing somewhat discomfited. "You give me more credit than I deserve. I do no more than would others in a like situation."

To Sinclair's vast relief, the maid entered the parlor bearing the tea tray, thus bringing about an end to the conversation—a conversation on a topic he'd no wish to pursue.

Supper at Berry House proved to be a jovial occasion. Freddie, released from his dread of prosecution, was full of high spirits. However, as his schoolboy jokes drew naught but a groaning response from his companions, he eventually contented himself with listening to the general flow of relaxed conversation.

"How long do you intend to stay in Buxton, Sinclair?" asked Phillip, offering up his wineglass to the maid so that it might be refilled.

"I believe it would be prudent to commence our journey on the morrow," replied the earl. "It would not do that we delay our return. We will travel separately, of course. Jenny and Freddie are to go to my sister's house, while I return to London."

Turning to Jennifer, Phillip smiled. "I will, of course, put myself at your disposal. I will escort you and Freddie to Ravensby." When Jenny would have protested, he shook his head. "I insist upon it. I can't allow you to career over the countryside in a hired chaise when I can provide the comforts of my own."

Jenny cast the earl a hasty glance. "There is absolutely no

need for your concern, Phillip," she replied. "Freddie and I will manage quite well."

"Come, Sinclair, support me in this," Rutledge demanded. "Don't you think it wise that I accompany them? Surely you see the sense of my suggestion."

"In truth, I do," replied the earl, "but I leave the decision to Jenny. Though one would suspect she has had a surfeit of hired vehicles."

"Could we not travel part of the way together, Ned?" she asked.

"I think not. We should be cautious and take separate routes if we're to maintain the ruse. Let Phillip accompany you. I will feel easier in my mind knowing you have an escort."

"What about me?" cried Freddie indignantly. "Am I of no account?"

"No!" came the laughing reply from his supper companions.

Later that evening, as the company prepared to retire, the earl and Jennifer found themselves seated alone in the parlor.

"I'm glad they've gone," said Jenny quietly. "It's so much more comfortable when there's only the two of us, Ned." She was silent for a moment, seeming to consider a point before she continued. "I realize now that I shouldn't have involved you in all of this, and I quite see the impropriety of the situation. I've placed you in an invidious position."

"Nonsense, my dear," he replied, leaving his seat and coming to sit beside her on the couch. "I've enjoyed our escapade enormously, but now is the time to bring it to its close."

"Are you sure Flora will not resent our being thrust so unceremoniously onto her generosity?"

He smiled reassuringly. "I have every confidence that she will welcome you with open arms. As I've explained, I know my sister well. She will be delighted to be made privy to our little venture. Indeed, I would guess she will be most disappointed *not* to have been included earlier."

Jenny chuckled. "If she had been included, there would not now be any need for subterfuge."

Sinclair smiled ruefully. "I love my sister dearly, but I positively refuse to travel half the country's length in her company. She chatters incessantly."

Jenny gave a small trill of laughter. "So do I."

"Yes, that thought had crossed my mind," he replied, grinning openly.

"You're laughing at me," she accused him with an irrepressible twinkle. "I dare say you find me amusing, but you will soon tire of your sport."

"I never tire of laughing."

"Wretch." She chuckled. Then, contritely, she asked, "Dear Edward, have I plagued you dreadfully?"

"Quite," he responded in a much altered tone, his mood taking a sudden change. She raised inquiring eyes to his, and for a moment he studied her face. "Jenny, I . . ." he began, but before his words could go further, his arm reached out of its own volition and drew her to him. Bowing his head, he tenderly kissed her with a poignant longing made all the more sweet by her tentative, naive response.

"Marry me, Jen," he whispered against her cheek when they finally drew apart.

"No . . . No . . . Please, Ned, there is no need," she cried, pulling away. "I quite understand your motives, and I am truly grateful. Because of what has been said, you feel you've compromised me, but indeed you have not. It's vastly obliging of you to offer for me, but I assure you, there's no need."

" 'Obliging' of me? What nonsense is this? Surely, you must realize . . ."

At that moment the parlor door was opened, and Freddie came quickly into the room, and whatever words the boy would have uttered, clearly died on his lips as he took in the scene before him.

The earl immediately came to his feet and, taking Jenny's hand, bowed over it. "Forgive me, my dear," he said quietly. "I forget myself. Have no fear—I will not embarrass you by repeating my indiscretion. You may be perfectly easy in my company when next we meet." Turning abruptly on his heel, he strode from the room, seeing not the bewildered look on her pale countenance.

Closing the door to his bedchamber, Sinclair placed the candle on the mantel and sat in the hearthside chair. Closing his eyes, he rested his head against the chair back, silently cursing himself for being a fool. He could not believe how close he'd come to revealing his closely guarded secret. It had not been his intention to utter a declaration; the words had come unbidden, and, witnessing Jenny's reaction, he wished them unsaid. He'd come within a hairsbreadth of forsaking his resolve to deny his emotions. It was a resolve he'd fought hard to control over the past days they'd spent together, and he inwardly cringed at what a fool he must have appeared.

Jenny had given no indication that she thought of him as anything other than a friend, and who could blame her? Certainly not he! He would not, could not, allow his feelings to rule him. He loved her too well. He could not believe, after valiantly concealing his deep affection for so long, how easily his barriers had been breached in that one unguarded moment.

He sat thus for some while, having no desire to retire, until eventually he went to his valise. Placing his hand inside, his fingers sought the portrait, but as they did not immediately encounter the silver frame, he took the candle and held it aloft. Still no portrait, and for a moment he couldn't comprehend its loss. All of a sudden the memory of placing it beneath his pillow the previous night came to him. With Jenny's arrival so early that morning and their hastened departure, he'd given it no thought, and a sense almost of panic overcame him. No matter what, he could not lose it; it was too precious to him. His instant thought was to return to the inn immediately, but he realized that would be foolish. However, he resolved to leave for The Sow's Ear at first light.

He undressed and lay in the bed, but repose would not come. Instead, he lay awake, his thoughts giving him no peace, until the first sign of dawn began to break, and he rose to make his preparations for departure.

The occupants of Berry House kept country hours and breakfasted early. When Jennifer arrived at the breakfast table, her pale countenance bore evidence that she, too, had spent a sleepless night.

"My dear, you look quite worn," said Judith with some concern. "Do you think yourself up to journeying today? Would it perhaps be wise to delay your return until the morrow?"

"No, we shall go today," replied Jenny, making no effort to attempt the meal set before her. Turning to Phillip, she asked, "Where's Edward? Is he not yet down?"

"He has been down and is gone," replied Phillip, oblivious to the edge in her voice. "He rose quite early and asked if he could have the use of one of my horses. Apparently he's left something of value at the last inn you visited and felt the need to retrieve it immediately."

"I would have gone with him, but he wouldn't have me," said a disappointed Freddie. "Said I was to go with you to Flora's."

"Did he leave any message for me?" asked Jenny, unease sounding in her voice.

"Only that he'll join you at Ravensby as soon as he's able," replied Phillip. "Sinclair's a strange fellow, if you ask me. He was quite curt this morning and abroad so early. It was barely dawn when he came to my door."

"Did he say what it was that he'd lost?" she asked, a small frown creasing her brow.

"Only that it was of value, though what it could be, I cannot think. If it was so valuable, why bring it on such a harebrained journey?"

"Will he return to Berry House?"

"No. He said he would have the horse returned to me and leave directly for London by post chaise."

Jenny rose from the table. "If you will excuse me, I will make my preparations for the journey," she said, a slight tremor in her voice, of which only Freddie seemed aware.

"We leave in an hour. Be ready," called Phillip to her retreating figure.

As she entered her bedchamber and attempted to close the door, Freddie pushed past her into the room. Standing before her with hands on hips, he demanded, "*Will* you tell me what this issue is between you and Sinclair? You refused to tell me last night, but surely you could confide it to me now. You know I won't breathe a word. Perhaps I can help."

"You can't," replied Jenny dejectedly. "No one can."

He put an arm about her shoulders, in that moment feeling much older than she. "You know I think he's a great gun. I can't believe he would wound you."

"He hasn't wounded me," she whispered, fighting back tears. "He offered for me."

"Excellent!" he responded, giving her shoulders a squeeze. "I knew the two of you would deal famously together. I thought it all along."

"I refused him!"

Freddie fell back in amazement. "I can't believe it. I always knew you were hen-witted. I thought so when you rejected him the first time. But why refuse him now?"

"He only offered out of a sense of duty," she said, wiping away her tears. "I couldn't accept him on those terms. Surely you must see that."

"It wasn't duty I saw on his face when I came on you last evening. Oh, Jenny, you can be such a . . . a . . . *female* at times. I may not know much, but this I can tell you: I truly believe he has an affection for you."

"Then that shows just how little you do know," she retorted, an irrational irritation rising. "He finds me amusing, nothing more."

"And what's your opinion of him?"

"He's insufferable, and I hate him." She felt no satisfaction whatsoever in saying those words, not understanding why they only served to make her feel even more wretched.

Chapter Seven

"Oh, aye, the portrait, my lord." The landlord of The Sow's Ear smiled when the earl questioned him in the tap-room of the inn. "The gentleman took it. Said he knew you and would return it to you immediately."

"What gentleman?" snapped Sinclair, a decided feeling of unease coming to bear.

"Why, he said he was a friend of your'n, sir. I didn't catch his name, but he said he knew you quite well. A very pleasant man, if I may say so."

"How was he aware of the portrait?"

"The maid brought it to me when he was paying his shot, and very interested he was in it too. Said he'd seen it afore."

Thoroughly perplexed, the earl frowned. "He gave no indication of his identity?"

"None, sir, only that he'd been to the races, where he sup-posed you and the young shaver to have been."

Sinclair cursed long and low, his mind attempting to iden-tify the half-hidden features of the figure on the stairs, but no recognition came. Forcing a smile, he said, "I thank you. Undoubtedly it will be returned to me when I reach London."

The journey to London seemed infinitely longer than had its predecessor, although in truth it was almost a day shorter, and the earl was relieved when the chaise finally halted outside Sinclair House. Once inside its portals, he lost no time inquiring whether any object or message had been left for him.

"Master Peregrine arrived from Oxford only this morning," stated the footman as he relieved his master of his curly-brimmed beaver. "Other than that, no, sir."

"And where's my brother now?" asked the earl, indicating that his valise should be taken to his apartment.

"I do believe he's gone to call on the Earl of Hawley, my lord."

The earl's dark eyebrows snapped into a heavy frown. "The stupid boy, whatever is he at now? How long has he been gone?"

Regarding the hall clock, the butler replied, "Almost three hours, sir."

"Then he could be anywhere by now," replied Sinclair in an exasperated tone. "I will go to my apartment to change. If he's not returned by the time I've accomplished the task, I shall require my coach."

Taking the stairs two at a time, the earl repaired immediately to his dressing room, calling for his valet as he went. Peregrine's arrival left him in no even mood, and he wondered exactly what his scapegrace brother was finding it necessary to impart to Hawley.

However, almost as soon as he'd been assisted off with his coat and boots, Perry burst unceremoniously into the dressing room.

Seeing the thunderous look that crossed his employer's countenance, the valet made a hasty retreat. He'd no desire to be privy to the altercation he felt sure was about to take place.

"Where the deuce have you been, Ned?" Perry demanded, standing in the center of the room, his usually pleasant countenance dark with a frown. "You've never heard such a hue and cry as your disappearance has set up. No one knew where you'd gone. Hawley has returned with me and is at this very moment installed in the drawing room. He's insisting you must know of his sister's whereabouts and demands that I contact you."

"Then you must inform him that you have found me and that I will be with him directly," replied Sinclair coldly. "However, before you do, you can tell me why you found it necessary to go to him with your tales, when Jenny and I have gone to such lengths to keep him in ignorance of Freddie's little escapade. Couldn't you have trusted me?"

"I didn't know you were involved in the matter," replied a contrite Perry. "Hawley thought it was all a hum, that you'd eloped with Jenny. Knew you wouldn't do it—told 'im so, but he wouldn't believe me. Fact is, the House Master has written to him about Freddie's disappearance, so I had to come to warn him and to tell him the truth."

"Then you might as well have done so in the first place instead of burdening Jenny with your problems," Sinclair scoffed.

"She came to you for help?" asked Perry.

"Obviously, as you should have done. Who else had she to turn to?"

"Then where is she? Has she returned? For if she has, I haven't seen her."

"I've sent her with Freddie to Flora. It's to appear that they'd gone into the country for a visit. You, my dear brother, are to join them there to add weight to their story."

"I must tell you, Ned, the tabbies lost no time in drawing conclusions at your joint disappearance and declared you to have eloped."

"Then they are destined for disappointment, are they not?"

"Is there no chance of a reconciliation between you?"

"None whatsoever!"

When they entered the drawing room a short while later, Hawley came immediately to his feet, crossing the distance between them to stand accusingly before the earl, his mean countenance flushed with anger.

"Where's Jennifer?" he demanded. "Don't try to fob me off with excuses, Sinclair. I know you've been in her company. Oh, it may not have been an elopement—I am well aware of the facts—but you've squired her to God knows where."

"To Buxton, to be precise," replied the earl calmly.

Hawley appeared incredulous. "Freddie's fled to Rutledge?"

"Exactly."

"And where are they now?"

"Rutledge has taken them to my sister in Essex."

"I suppose you will expect me to believe that your association with my sister was quite innocent. That you were in her company the whole while and behaved with absolute propriety?" sneered Hawley.

"If you believe our association to have been anything other than that of the highest moral standing, then it would prove how little you know of your sister and our relationship."

"Whatever the truth of your relationship, you must know that, in the eyes of the world, you have ruined her."

The earl sat on a corner of his desk, negligently swinging one booted foot. Despite a valiant effort to maintain his equilibrium, he nonetheless eyed Hawley with complete distaste, saying, "Then, as her brother, it's in your interest to offer support and help allay the gossip. If it's seen that you endorse our explanation and declare her visit to Flora genuine, who would dare proclaim it a lie?"

"I don't like it. I don't like it by half," said Hawley, sitting heavily in a chair. "When you state it so plainly, it seems too simple. By all that's right, you should be bound in honor to marry her."

"She would not have me," stated Sinclair coldly.

"You made her an offer?" asked Hawley, incredulous.

"I did, and she refused."

Hawley came quickly to his feet. "Then we shall see what she has to say on the subject when *I* speak to her. I will not allow her to relinquish such an opportunity."

Perry was taken aback by the hardness that came over his brother's countenance, the like of which he had never before witnessed.

"You will not coerce her into marriage with me or any other of your choosing," seethed Sinclair, also rising and taking a step toward his antagonist. "And if it's made known that you make life difficult for her, I can assure you, you will not find her without support."

"Yourself?" scoffed Hawley.

"Precisely!"

"Then you are a bigger fool than I gave you credit for, Sinclair. You champion a lost cause."

Involuntarily the earl's hand shot out, seizing Hawley's neck-cloth, snatching him forward until he was but inches from his face, his toes teetering on the floor. Perry took a quick step toward them but at a warning look from Sinclair fell back, feeling naught but an onlooker at the scene being enacted before him.

Tightening his hold until Hawley clawed at his neck for air, Sinclair gave a hard laugh. "You have no liking for intimidation, do you, Hawley?" he mocked. "It seems more your style to be dispensing it to defenseless females. Not so keen when you are the recipient, are you?"

In response, Hawley gave a spluttered reply, but his words were lost in his need for air as he struggled to keep his balance.

Sinclair issued a harsh oath and, relinquishing his hold, thrust him roughly away. Perry came to stand at his side, but the earl appeared oblivious to his presence. Watching Hawley's attempt to regain his composure, it was a moment before he again spoke.

"I trust that when next we meet, I need not remind you of caution toward your sister," he warned as Hawley edged his way to the door. "I would not wish it to be necessary to repeat my admonition."

Having no desire to prolong the interview, red-faced and seething, Hawley made good his escape. Roundly cursing Jennifer for the stupidity he perceived to be the cause of his humiliation, he consoled himself with the promise that he would repay Sinclair for his treatment at the first opportunity.

"Never knew you could be so ruthless, Ned," breathed Perry, as, going to a side table, the earl poured himself a glass of brandy and tossed back its contents.

"Then take care that I don't turn my anger against you and your idiotic friend," snapped Sinclair, finding it difficult to relinquish his mood. "If you'd applied more common sense to the situation, none of this would have come about."

Perry had the grace to bow his head. This was a side to his brother he had never before seen, and it was alien to him. "I'm sorry, Ned," he said penitently. "I tried to resolve it myself— believe me, I did—but . . ." Words failed him.

Full of contrition, the earl came to lay his arm about his brother's shoulders. "I, too, am sorry," he said. "I shouldn't take my frustration out on you. Indeed, it is unpardonable of me. I thought I'd come to terms with my life and planned the way forward. I was not prepared for the confusion that would be left to rule."

"I don't understand your meaning," said Perry, much perplexed.

Sinclair grimaced. "It's as well that you don't. There's too much at issue, and it would be unforgivable of me to burden you with it."

"Am I to go to Ravensby alone, Ned, or will you accompany me?"

"You must go alone. I need remain here for a while. There's a matter I need attend to before I join you there, though how it will be resolved, I don't know."

"Can you confide it to me? Perhaps I could help," said Perry hopefully.

"I wish that you could, but I've lost something that belongs to me and don't know how to retrieve it."

"Is it valuable?"

"To me, yes, very."

"What is it, Ned?"

"Something that's very difficult to define. A talisman, an amulet, a charm. Some would say a lifesaver. Call it what you will, but it's something I've carried with me for some time, and while it's of very little monetary value, to me it's priceless."

Still no wiser, Perry decided it would be prudent to let the matter rest.

As the earl had predicted, Flora eagerly welcomed Jennifer and Freddie to her home and, when the story was told, stated herself more than willing to help. Phillip, although aware that pressing matters awaited him in Buxton—at Carlton's invitation, which had been merely issued out of politeness—stayed on at Ravensby. He received no encouragement whatsoever from Jennifer, but, being now confirmed that her prior betrothal was indeed at an end, he was as determined as ever to press his own cause.

"I declare, you and Edward thoroughly mystify me," stated Flora when she and Jenny sat alone in the morning room at Ravensby. "There always appears some issue between you, and yet you profess no attachment. I am thoroughly confused."

"Then you needn't be," said Jenny with a little twisted smile. "Edward remains protective toward me, that is all."

"And you toward him?"

"Oh, he's a good friend," she replied nonchalantly, "and he has proved he would go to any lengths, however distasteful, to shield me. When the impropriety of his having accompanied me to Buxton was pointed out to him, his immediate reaction was to offer me the protection of his name."

Flora appeared much taken aback. "You say he offered for you? I am bewildered. He's frequently assured me that he's determined not to renew the engagement and has taken great pains to declare his intention of never marrying. Am I not to believe a word he utters? For I tell you, none would be more delighted than I to see the two of you make a match of it."

"Then I'm afraid you will be sadly disappointed. He thought only to save me from the scandalmongers, and I would not allow him to make such a sacrifice on my behalf. I'm sure you can see that I couldn't allow it. No thoughts of marriage had crossed his mind until Judith and Phillip Rutledge found it necessary to comment on the impropriety of our journey. Until that point we had been quite comfortable in each other's company. Indeed, I was saddened that our expedition had reached its conclusion, as, I believed, was Ned."

"Could you not have found it in your heart to accept him, my dear?" asked Flora, laying her hand over Jenny's and giving it a gentle squeeze.

"My heart has nothing whatsoever to do with it," stated Jenny, rising hastily and declaring her intention of seeking out Freddie.

"That is where you are very wrong, my dear," whispered Flora to the empty room. "So very wrong."

Later that evening, when Flora and Carlton sat cozily ensconced in her boudoir, she sighed and confided in him, "Even though she tries so hard to disguise it, I'm sure the chit is in love with Edward. I do believe she has even managed to fool herself into believing she's indifferent to him."

"Whatever the right of it, you must allow them to take their own course," replied Carlton, becoming somewhat bored with the topic and endeavoring to channel his wife's thoughts in his own direction. "You know I hold your brother in the highest esteem, but I believe he is quite capable of ordering his own life, and I'm certain he would not welcome your meddling in his affairs. Couldn't you confine your energies to more immediate tasks? Am I forever to vie with him for your attention?"

"Fie on you, my love. You know my thoughts are always of you." She chuckled, patting his cheek.

"Then I would appreciate proof of that fact," he replied, taking her into his arms.

The news that the Earl of Sinclair had returned to London—alone—permeated society, and the inevitable comments were

made. Those who claimed to know him well endorsed the belief that he had indeed been out of town on an expedition to
the races. However, a tenacious few still refused to believe
that as fact and clung to the conviction that his absence was
most definitely connected to the disappearance of the heiress,
even though her brother stated that she was at that very moment visiting Lady Flora Carlton in Essex. So convinced remained certain individuals that they actually dared accost
Sinclair with their theory, but with a great effort he managed
to retain his composure and brush their questions aside in a
most convincing manner. Lord Melville, being one of their
numbers, showed a great relief at the explanation that Jennifer
was at present staying with Lady Carlton and eagerly promised to quell any further rumors when the affair was mentioned in his presence.

As several days passed, the earl became aware of an almost
overwhelming desire to go to Ravensby as he'd promised, but
as there had been no signs of the portrait being restored to
him, he dared not leave London, should he, in his absence,
miss its return.

Arriving home at noon after a morning spent at Horse
Guards, the earl was informed by the footman that Sgt. Randall
had called and, finding Sinclair not at home, had stated his intention of returning later in the day. The earl searched his memory but could call no sergeant of that name to mind. Indeed, he
could remember no one of that name in his company, so it was
with some perplexity that he awaited his arrival.

He didn't have long to wait. No sooner had he risen from a
light luncheon and repaired to the library than he was informed
of Randall's arrival. Almost immediately a small, wiry individual was issued into his presence. Marching smartly up to
the earl's desk, he saluted, his actions appearing incongruous,
dressed as he was in the garb of a dandy. Looking up from the
papers he had been examining, the earl came quickly to his
feet, seeing before him the face from the inn.

"Sergeant Anthony Randall of the Twenty-ninth Regiment of Foot, sir," said the dandy, maintaining the salute.

"We are no longer in the military, Randall. There's no need to salute me," said the earl, resuming his seat and indicating that his visitor should take the chair facing the desk. Then, coming immediately to the point, he asked, "Do I take it that your arrival has some connection to the portrait I have mislaid?"

"It has, sir," said Randall, reaching into his pocket to retrieve the very object that had been the cause of such great concern and laying it on the desk before him.

Resisting the impulse to immediately snatch it up, the earl leaned back in his chair. "I am exceedingly grateful to you for its return. Your face is vaguely familiar to me and yet not your name. Should I know you?" he asked with some perplexity.

Randall studied a point above the earl's head, appearing to bring the memory to mind. "We've met on two previous occasions, though I hardly think you will remember, sir. The first occasion I will never forget—it was when we fought the French at Albuera. There was a lot of smoke on the battlefield, our cannon and their cannon blasting powder and shot by the ton. It was blinding. The French came out of the smoke in a column and marched toward us, their kettledrums pounding. My men fired volley after volley, but still they came, but my boys held until they smashed into our lines like a hammer and we thought all was lost. Suddenly, out of the smoke, rode Marchant's Cavalry, and I saw you lead your men in the attack.

"You were a sight to behold that day, sir. No one could have burst through that smoke with more fury than you. Not even Old Nick himself. Your men followed hard on your heels. You had two horses taken from under you during the battle, and still you fought like a demon. . . ."

"You spoke of a second meeting," interrupted the earl coldly, obviously having no liking for the recollection.

"Ah, our second meeting was not quite so glorious," sighed Randall, returning his gaze. "It was in the field hospital after Salamanca and in the convent for a short while afterward. They really thought you were done for, sir, but I told 'em you were a fighter. Couldn't help but notice how you clung to the little portrait. We all saw that it did you good. . . ."

"That may be," interrupted the earl once more. "Now tell me, how did you come to be at The Sow's Ear?"

"Well, sir, because of my injuries I couldn't continue in the Twenty-ninth, which meant I must find myself a civilian profession. But that was not easy, as there were so many others in a like situation. Eventually I turned to Bow Street, and I became a constable—a runner—call it what you will. When you saw me at The Sow's Ear, I was working incognito, so to speak. Hence my current mode of dress." He grinned, indicating his foppish garb. "Not at all to my liking, I assure you, but we were on the trail of a thief who targets such gentlemen as yourself. Hence my need for disguise."

"You say 'we.' You were not alone at the inn?"

"No, sir, I had two other constables working with me, but you didn't see them. They were in the taproom at the time of our encounter."

"Was it you who came to my door in the night?"

"No, sir, it was our quarry."

"And to my companion's door?"

"Again the quarry. But have no fear—we had him under close watch at all times. Your 'companion' was never in any danger. We arrested our man at daybreak and relieved him of the evidence of his guilt. He now faces quite a hefty term in jail or even deportation to the Americas."

Smiling, the earl came to his feet and extended his hand, taking Randall's in a firm grasp. "Then I must thank you for keeping my portrait and my 'companion' safe," he said. "You will be well rewarded, I assure you."

"I want no reward," affirmed Randall, also coming to his feet and taking the hand offered. "It is an honor to serve you, sir." Then, after a moment's pause, he added, "However, there is one thing I would ask of you, my lord, if I may."

"Ask."

"Should you hear of anyone requiring a steward or agent or

some such, would you bear me in mind? I've no liking for the law."

"I have need of a steward at Fly Hall," said Sinclair.

Randall's plain countenance broke into a hesitant smile. "Do you manufacture the post for me? I wouldn't wish you to feel obligated, sir. It was not my intention in returning your property to you."

"It is certainly not manufactured," lied the earl, "and I would welcome someone with your loyalty in my employ. Such a man is rare."

Much pleased with the outcome of the interview, Randall took his leave so that he could make his arrangements to travel to Fly Hall.

Left alone, the earl examined the portrait, relief flooding his senses at its return. Assuring himself that it had received no harm during its absence, he whispered, "So, at last you are returned to me, my love. I can't tell you what it cost me when I thought I'd lost you. All else is in turmoil, yet you remain the same. I don't know how I would have borne your loss." Rising, he left the library, and, returning the miniature to its resting place in his bedchamber, he determined to travel to Ravensby on the morrow.

As the earl sat alone over supper, he heard a commotion in the hall, and just as he was about to inquire of its origins, Perry burst into the room, his disheveled appearance proclaiming a hurried journey.

"I thought I told you to stay with Flora until I came to you," said Sinclair, turning in his chair to face the newcomer.

"It's that damned Rutledge," stated Perry hotly, defiance showing in his every line. "I can't stand his pompous ways. He's forever ordering me about. Why, a chap can't even take the dogs out to find game of a morning without his wanting to know where I was going and what I was doing. If you ask me, he's addlepated, bats in his belfry."

"Rutledge remains at Ravensby?" asked Sinclair, incredulous.

"I was of the opinion he would have returned to Buxton by now."

"Oh, aye, that was his intention right and tight, but damn me if he didn't find it necessary to wheedle an invitation out of Carlton to stay. The poor man could scarcely refuse without seeming disagreeable. Rutledge is falling over himself to pay attention to Jenny, and you can see she doesn't want it. The only one pleased to see him stay was Freddie, and even his patience wears thin. Even he can't abide his forever keeping tracks on us. We're not still in short coats, yet that's how he treats us. Flora's in one hell of a tiz. Wants to know when you're coming down. States she's had enough of the fellow."

"It had been my intention to travel down on the morrow, but perhaps it would be more prudent of me to await his departure."

"If you do, Ned, Flora will never forgive you." Perry grinned, seating himself at the table and helping himself to the fruit in the bowl in its center. "Carlton's taken himself off to God knows where, and she swears it's because Rutledge remains. Perhaps if you were to present yourself, he'd return to Buxton."

"Jenny may not be so pleased if he does; they appear to deal extremely well together."

"Not so well that it shows at the moment. She appears quite downcast. We even offered to drive her to the old ruins, but she showed no interest."

"What, not interested in a pile of old stones? I can't believe it," mocked the earl.

"You may laugh," reproved Perry, "but we only wanted to cheer her up. Take her away from Rutledge, so she didn't have to listen to his interminable prosing."

Returning to Ravensby after an afternoon's ride in the company of his sister and Phillip Rutledge, Freddie Lynton quickly drew rein and pointed an imperative finger toward the stables as a team of matching bays were led across its yard.

"They're Ned's—I'm sure of it! I'd know them anywhere,"

he cried enthusiastically, and, urging his horse to a canter, he headed in their direction, Jennifer doing likewise.

Having no desire to follow in their wake, Rutledge held back, cursing roundly. An unreasoning anger overtook him at thought of Sinclair's arrival, and he turned his horse away, desiring to prolong his ride. He most certainly had no wish to greet the earl. Knowing that Jenny had been awaiting his arrival, he saw his coming as an intrusion.

However, if Jennifer had been awaiting his arrival, she was determined not to show it. Instead of going immediately, as Freddie had done, to the rear salon, where the earl and his brother sat taking tea with Flora, she took her leisurely time in changing before making her presence known.

"My lord, how delightful to see you," she said nonchalantly upon entering the room and extending her hand as he rose to greet her.

He frowned slightly at the formal greeting but bowed briefly over her hand and attempted to mirror her indifferent mood.

Freddie had long since disappeared in the company of Perry, and Flora looked between the two, not knowing what to make of their reunion. They stood facing each other, saying nothing and appearing ill at ease. Seeing their awkwardness and not wishing to intrude, she made her exit on the pretext of ordering supper.

Being left alone had the desired effect of loosening Jenny's tongue, but the words were not what Flora would have expected. "You left me without a word, Edward Thurston," she accused him. "Surely I deserved better than that."

"Sit down, Jen, and I will explain," he cajoled, attempting to take her hand, but she snatched it away, hiding it behind her rose-colored skirts.

"I thought we'd come to a better understanding than that you should treat me in such a cavalier fashion," she said accusingly.

"I'm sure you wouldn't have thanked me for knocking on your door at dawn, for that is when I left for the inn."

"What was this *thing* that you'd lost and was so valuable that it necessitated your immediate departure?"

"A keepsake," he answered defensively. "Something that need not bother you—indeed, would not interest you."

"How do you know what would interest me?"

"Jen," he cajoled, "you are being quite unreasonable. Come, can we not cry truce?"

"I will cry truce when you tell me why you've found it necessary to remain in London for so long when you promised to come to Ravensby as soon as you could. Phillip was sure something or *someone* of more interest had sidetracked you."

"We are squabbling again, Jen." He chuckled. "How is it that, when I'm in your company, we are reduced to the role of schoolchildren? We sound like babes arguing over a toy."

"I'm sorry, Ned," she said contritely, her voice uneven, "but I've been waiting for you for what seems an eternity, and Phillip insisted that you'd no wish to return. He was adamant that you'd forgotten me. What could I think?"

He had the desire to put his arm about her to comfort her but was acutely aware of her reaction to his embrace at their last meeting and instead, managing to capture her hand, led her to the chaise, seating himself at her side.

"Rutledge could not be more mistaken," he said quietly, "and if I've offended you, I wholeheartedly apologize. I've spoken to Hawley, and I do believe that, between us, we have succeeded in averting a scandal. Some may still have their suspicions, but when they see that we don't seek each other's company, even those will vanish."

"Was Arthur *very* difficult?" she asked tentatively, wincing at thoughts of what her brother's reaction would have been when approached by Sinclair.

"Shall we say that after *discussion,* we reached an acceptable understanding? He knows all but recognizes it would be foolish to attempt to broadcast the facts or to attempt to force us into marriage. You will be welcomed home."

"Oh," she answered flatly.

"These arrangements don't sit well with you? You desire something different?"

"Yes . . . No . . . I don't know," she replied, seeming confused. "Flora has invited me to stay at Ravensby until Carlton returns and then to travel to London with them."

"And it is what you wish to do?"

"I believe so. It's preferable to returning to Arthur for the moment. I've a liking for Flora, and it will allow my elder brother more time to cool his temper."

A silence fell, and it was a moment before the earl became aware that Jennifer appeared to be distracted.

"What troubles you, Jen?" he asked solicitously. "Don't tell me 'tis nothing, for I can see it clearly on your face."

She turned fully to face him and took his hand in both of hers. "I wanted to thank you, Ned," she said solemnly. "You've been so good and kind to me, even offering for me when it's not at all what you wish."

He would have spoken, but she laid two fingers on his lips. "Please, say nothing," she implored. "Let me thank you. I may not have the chance again. I thrust myself upon you. Indeed, I allowed you no option other than to accompany me. If I had had my true deserts, you would have sent me packing, but you were ever the gentleman. Many in a like situation would have attempted to take advantage of it, but you did not. Phillip has pointed out to me that I behaved like a hoyden, and I believe he is right. I never thought of the position I was putting you in. As he says, I acted no better than an opera girl. . . ."

"Damn Rutledge," swore Sinclair passionately. "What right has he to judge your actions?"

"I believe every right," said a pompous voice from the doorway as Phillip sauntered in, slowly drawing off his riding gloves. "In fact, I am ever hopeful that Jenny will become my wife. Therefore, my comments are quite within keeping. I foresee no opposition from Hawley. In truth, it will resolve a very awkward situation, and I see no reason for him to issue a refusal."

"No!" cried Jenny, coming quickly to her feet. "I've told you, I have no intention of marrying anyone."

A look of insufferable superiority flitted across Phillip's haughty countenance. "We will see how long that intent lasts when you are confronted by censure at every turn, my dear. Indeed, we will see what Hawley has to say on the subject."

"Arthur will have no say in the matter," replied Jennifer hotly, "and neither will you, Phillip. I order my own life."

The earl, too, came to his feet, but she pushed past him, and, casting Rutledge a look of complete dislike, she ran from the room.

"There's no need to cast me such darkling looks, Sinclair," sneered Rutledge, advancing into the room and depositing his length in a hearthside chair. "You had your chance—now it's mine. Have no fear, she will soon come about and see the sense of accepting me—I'm sure of it. We've dealt so well together in the past, I'm certain we will do so again."

"You are very confident of something that is far less than certain," replied Sinclair coldly. "You issue censure where none is warranted. The child is far too innocent. She saw no impropriety in seeking my aid, and the thought that it could be misconstrued never entered her head. If you must apportion blame, lay it at my door. It is I who should have had more sense."

"You had a great deal of sense, my friend—sense enough to know that if you compromised her, she would be obliged to marry you."

The earl strode toward Rutledge, his face dark with anger, his hand clenched at his side. "If my desire was to marry her, I would not stoop to trickery to achieve my ends. I have the sense not to attempt to coerce her into a disastrous marriage. I would take no unwilling bride, but you obviously would not balk at the thought."

"Then we shall see how unwilling she is once she has returned to London," sneered Rutledge, rising and moving away. "She will soon realize that even an heiress is not allowed to flaunt the laws of propriety." Watching his companion, he liked not the look on the earl's severe countenance. It came to him that it would not serve his purpose to enter into a situation over which he had no certain control, a situation that could remove his influence over Jennifer. He was no fool. To remain would give her the opportunity to draw comparisons, and he was far from confident of the result.

"I see that I am no longer required here," he said with an air of superiority. "I remained merely to ensure that Jennifer would be well received by your sister. I've matters to attend to in Buxton. However, be assured, I do not relinquish my claim. I have every intention of pursuing my cause, and we will see the outcome of this little dispute when I return to London."

"Then we will not keep you longer from your home," replied the earl. "I can assure you, there's no further need for your concern. Be assured that she is quite well received and no longer requires your company. Indeed, the hour is not so far advanced that you need delay your departure. I believe you may attain a good thirty miles before you are required to put up for the night."

Rutledge colored profusely. He was not used to being the recipient of such forthright animosity, but he was no fool. "I believe, as you suggest, I will make my departure immediately. I've no wish to be *de trop*." He made a move toward the door but halted, briefly turning to face his companion. Making a short bow, he said tersely, "I would be obliged if you would thank our hostess for her hospitality and inform her of my departure."

"I can assure you, we are *devastated* by your loss," mocked the earl, watching his retreat with distinct satisfaction.

The candles burned low in their sconces, but still sleep would not come. Finally Jennifer rose from her bed and, wrapping her silk robe about her, went to sit in the chair by the hearth.

She had been relieved to hear of Phillip's departure but saw it as only prolonging the situation, for she knew he would return to attempt to coerce her into accepting his proposal. She had no doubt that his affection for her was genuine, but, meeting him again after an absence of more than three years, she realized that her memories of him had been somewhat distorted. She'd remembered him as an affable friend, liking not the arrogant being he'd now become, and she realized that his manner contrasted most unfavorably to that of the earl.

Even now, as she sat alone in her chamber, she wasn't prepared to admit the turmoil into which Sinclair's arrival at Ravensby had pitched her emotions, indeed had done since his return from war. She'd been so certain of her decision to end the betrothal before his arrival, but now . . .

"I hate you, Edward Thurston," she confided to the dying embers in the hearth before retreating to her bed once more.

No sooner had her head rested on the pillow than she heard a cry from one of the adjoining bedchambers, quickly followed by yet another, and immediately she was on her feet, drawing on her wrap, for she'd recognized that voice.

Running into the corridor, she was met by Perry holding aloft a candle as he, too, ran to the earl's door, and, thrusting it wide, they entered. Sinclair lay in the vast bed, mumbling incoherently in his sleep, appearing much agitated. He wore no nightshirt, and they saw that his brow and powerful chest were soaked in sweat.

"Close the door," commanded Perry quietly, placing the candle on the bedside table. "Ned sometimes has these dreams. They are less frequent now than at the beginning but no less violent."

The candle cast flickering shadows over Sinclair's face, revealing that his eyes were wide, but he obviously still slept. Suddenly his words became audible, as, raising himself up, he issued battlefield commands in an urgent voice.

"What can we do?" cried Jenny, as Perry attempted to press his brother back onto the pillows. Sinclair only became more agitated in the attempt, issuing oaths and gripping Perry's arm in a viselike hold. "Shall I call Flora?" she asked, making for the door.

"Leave Flora be," replied a much-concerned Perry. "She

only goes into a flap and is no use in these situations. We must ride it out. He would become confused and disorientated should we attempt to wake him."

Quickly looking about the room, Jennifer spied the ewer left on the dresser for the earl's refreshment and, taking up one of the fine linen towels, soaked it in the cool water. Returning to the bed, she attempted to place it on his fevered brow, but again he became more violent and pushed her away.

"Go back to bed," said Perry. "I will sit with him. We can do nothing more."

"I believe if we could just cool him, he would fare much better," stated Jenny. "Here, take the cloth and sponge his chest."

Perry did as he was bid, talking to his brother all the while, attempting to soothe him while Jenny took his hand in a reassuring clasp, not so much as flinching when his fingers tightened unbearably on hers.

Eventually he fell back onto the pillows, his ranting reduced to an agitated mumbling. Among the confusion of words, Jennifer frequently distinguished the word *portrait.*

"What is this portrait he appears so concerned about?" she asked Perry when she was able. "It seems uppermost in his mind."

"He carries a miniature with him, though I've never seen it. Indeed, he doesn't know I'm aware of its existence, but I came across him examining it in his bedchamber one evening, and he quickly hid it."

"Does he have it with him now? Do you think it would calm him?"

Perry searched the drawers and closet, but no portrait could be found.

Suddenly Jenny became aware that the mumbling had ceased and that the earl's eyes had taken on a look of recognition.

"Jen?" he whispered, as if scarcely believing her presence. "Is that you, Jen?" Releasing his hand from her clasp, he raised himself once more to a sitting position and rubbed his fingers across his forehead in a bemused way. "I've been dreaming again," he offered in explanation. "Have I woken you? Is that

Perry skulking in the shadows? Have I woken the whole house?"

"No, only Perry and me," assured Jenny, pushing him once more back against the pillows.

"You must think me feeble-brained." He grimaced.

"Certainly not, though we were greatly concerned for you."

"Then you need not be," he continued. "I suffer from night terrors, nothing more. They're not as violent as they once were and are far less frequent, but I don't know when to expect them or what activates them."

"You appeared troubled about a portrait," said Jenny, taking up the cloth, at last being able to bathe his brow. "Tell us where it can be found, and we will bring it to you. Perry was looking for it when you awoke. . . ."

"No!" he almost shouted, and she feared he was becoming agitated again. "There is no portrait. Let it be."

Perry came to stand at the foot of the bed. "Can I get you anything, Ned? A brandy perhaps?"

"Thank you. I would welcome a glass of brandy," said Sinclair wearily.

As Perry left the room, Jennifer rose to leave, but the earl caught her hand. "Will you not stay for a moment, Jen?" he asked. "Sit with me a little." She resumed her seat at the side of the bed.

"Did I frighten you?" he asked quietly. "For you must know that I'm not aware of what I say when the terror overtakes me, and I would not wish to alarm or offend you."

"You have certainly not offended me in any way, but I was concerned for you. The battles have left you with very vivid recollections, and the horrors of war are firmly imprinted on your memory. Who should blame you for your terrors?"

He smiled with an effort and took her hand in a warm clasp, his eyelids suddenly appearing heavy. "You are very understanding, my dear," he mumbled as he drifted into sleep.

Watching his features soften in repose, Jenny, for the first time, allowed her gaze to study the paling scars that crisscrossed his side, and tears blurred her vision. Tentatively she traced their course with one gentle finger. "Oh, how they have hurt you, my love," she breathed, resisting the urge to press her lips to the hard ridges where the flesh had healed. Before she could explore her emotions further, Perry entered with the glass of brandy, and she raised a finger to her lips and indicated that they should leave.

It was not until she herself had retired to bed that the thought struck her that the earl had shown no discomfiture at her seeing his scarring as he had done at The Sow's Ear, proving he felt more at ease with her. The thought pleased her enormously. However, when she thought of it, she admitted she was curious to know of the portrait and why it was so important to him.

Chapter Eight

"Why didn't you wake me?" complained Flora over breakfast the following morning.

"There was no need. Jenny was with me," replied Perry, attacking the sirloin placed before him with some vigor.

"The poor girl must have wondered what was happening. No wonder she wishes to breakfast in her apartment this morning."

"Jenny was more than equal to the task," scoffed Perry. "*She* doesn't indulge in histrionics,"

"Am I to take it, then, that you are inferring that I do?" asked Flora waspishly. "For I tell you . . ."

"I only state the truth." Perry grinned.

"Then 'tis excessively unkind of you to infer that I resort to dramatics. I would have been equally as able to attend to dear Edward."

"Oh, take a damper, Flo," Perry teased, scarcely pausing in the consumption of his meal.

Flora turned an indignant shade of pink. "Don't call me that. You know I can't abide it, you wretched boy."

"Bickering again, Perry?" remonstrated the earl, entering the room and coming to sit at the table. "Must you always find it necessary to torment our hostess, you ungrateful cub, especially when she has been gracious enough to take us all under her wing and offer her hospitality? There are few who would be so willing to open their doors to all and sundry."

"But then, my dear Ned, *you* are not all and sundry," replied a much mollified Flora. "My door is ever open to you,"

"But will not be to this young wretch." The earl chuckled. "Especially if he doesn't mind his manners. Apologize to your sister, you ungrateful pup."

An unrepentant Perry grudgingly issued a mumbled apology but was saved from further recriminations by the appearance of his friend at the door. Freddie Lynton, who'd breakfasted some while earlier, appeared in the doorway and with beckoning hand urged his friend to join him in the search for sport.

Alone in her apartment, Jenny sat pensively over her meal. Her curiosity had been whetted, and she desired nothing more than to know of this portrait that seemed so imperative to the earl. Had it been her imagination, or did he appear to become defensive when it was mentioned the previous night? Yet how could she broach the subject to him without incurring his wrath?

She'd heard him leave his apartment a short while earlier, and the thought came to her that she could go to his room while he was at his morning meal. Perhaps she might succeed where Perry had failed in locating it, but she pushed the thought away as soon as it had arisen. She would not serve him in such a cavalier manner. However, curiosity was a strange thing, raising all manner of possibilities in the mind, and she knew she would not be easy until she knew whose portrait it was that he so fiercely protected.

All of a sudden she remembered their meeting as he'd left the frame-maker's shop and she'd taken him up into her phaeton. When she thought back to that day, she was convinced that it was no portrait of his grandsire that had required re-framing. However, the alternative proved too painful to con-template. The thought that it was the face of a paramour that he studied refused to be dismissed, and she pushed away her cup so forcefully that its contents spilled upon the cloth.

Dabbing at the stain with her napkin, she felt an inexplicable vexation start to rise, and, leaving the table, she went to the window.

There she sat with her chin resting in her hand, watching the daily workings of the stable yard below, until a movement in the farthest corner caught her eye and she watched with some fascination as the earl mounted a large blood-chestnut. It was not the effortless grace with which he sat the spirited mount that drew her attention but his ability to appear as one with the horse, and for a moment she watched him with an ir-resistible fascination as he calmed the lively animal and en-couraged it to walk more steadily from the yard. As the maid arrived, on a thought, she quickly rose from her seat and asked her to lay out her riding habit.

Once settled in the saddle of a pretty gray mare, Jenny inquired of the earl's direction.

"I believe my lord to have ridden over to The Folly," in-formed the groom who'd assisted her to mount. "Do you re-quire me to accompany you on your ride, my lady?"

"There's no need. I am to join with his lordship," she replied, and, turning her mare, she, too, headed out of the yard.

Ravensby's grounds were extensive, but she knew the path that would take her to The Folly, and she urged the mare to a canter, soon leaving the formal gardens behind.

Finding herself riding through a small coppice, she slowed her pace to concentrate on the various twists and turns the path took, oblivious that she was being observed, almost cry-ing out in alarm when the earl drew the chestnut across her path.

"I give you good day, my lady." He grinned mischievously, bowing low in the saddle.

"Edward, you startled me," she cried reprovingly. "I had thought you gone to The Folly."

"I took a slight detour," he said, a note of amusement still lingering in his voice. "Dare I suggest that you were following me?"

"And why should I be following you?"

"I thought *you* might be inclined to tell *me*." He smiled, drawing his mount alongside the mare, and indicated that they should proceed along the path together.

"I merely decided to ride out," she replied haughtily. " 'Tis only your conceit that suggests it to be otherwise."

Sinclair's eyes sparkled. "Won't you allow me my conceit, Jen? I'm so rarely allowed to give it rein."

"Then you may give it rein, dear Ned." She chuckled, unable to resist the amusement in his eyes. "Yes, I admit I sought you out."

" 'Tis so gratifying when one is found to be right." He grinned, feigning hauteur.

"Your vanity does you no credit," she said, laughing and urging the mare to a canter as they emerged from the trees and The Folly came into sight.

The Folly was a marble summerhouse built on the lines of a Grecian temple. It stood in the midst of abundant foliage and was set on a small hill at the head of a steep flight of stone steps. Dismounting and tethering the horses, they started up the steps, the earl taking Jennifer's elbow to assist her ascent.

"The views are quite remarkable when we reach the top," he assured her. "Carlton's grandsire ordered it built for his wife, who was wont to spend her days reading there."

"I should have liked to meet him," said Jenny thoughtfully. "He must have loved her very much to order such a commission merely so that she could read in comfort."

"I doubt it was for the reading alone that he built it—more, I would say, to pay her homage. He was reputed to have doted on her."

"And your grandsire, Ned, did he dote on his wife, do you think?"

"Hardly." He grinned. "If my father was to be believed, she was a veritable harridan. She came over from France when her father fell foul of La Pompadour and Louis ordered him banished."

"I would have liked to meet her too." Jenny chuckled. "And your grandsire. Indeed, I would be very interested to see the portrait of him that you had reframed."

They had achieved the top of the steps and entered the summerhouse, but he stopped abruptly just within its door. "Why this sudden interest in portraits?" he asked, maintaining his hold on her arm and turning her about to face him. "What is it that fascinates you so about them?"

"I don't know what you mean," she replied, refusing to meet his gaze. "I merely show an interest in your family."

"Oh, aye, my family is so *very* interesting," he mocked. "Was it a family portrait you showed such interest in last night?"

She did look at him then, her blue eyes turning defiant. "I don't know, Ned. That is for you to tell me. It was you who asked for it in your delirium and seemed to have such need of it. How am I to know whose likeness it is?"

"I tell you, I have no portrait."

"Then, sir, you lie."

"You would call me a liar?"

"Most certainly, Edward. Indeed, I believe it to be of your sweetheart, your paramour."

"And what sweetheart is this that you accuse me so readily of? Just how likely am I to have a paramour?"

"As likely as any other man!"

He looked at her pityingly. "And you would honestly have me think you believe that?"

"Of course. What else am I to think?"

He relinquished his hold on her arm, his features turning harsh within the shadowed light of the summerhouse. "You, my dear, can think whatever you wish. I will not feed your curiosity." Turning toward the door, he made to leave, but her hastily spoken words halted him.

"Ned, I must know. Did you offer for me out of a sense of honor? Did you feel obligated to offer marriage?"

She saw his shoulders stiffen, and his tone was cold when, without turning, he answered, "If that is what you truly believe, you silly girl, then yes. If that explanation satisfies you, and it is how you perceive it, yes."

"Edward Thurston, I . . ." she began, but he was gone, his ears deaf to her words, and, sinking down onto the stone bench, she gave vent to her feelings of despondency.

Hastening down the flight of steps, Sinclair had almost achieved the pathway where the waiting horses were tethered when his pace faltered, and, on impulse, he turned, placing his foot on an upward course. But he knew that if he returned, his resolve would be as nothing, and he would be lost. Turning once more, he descended to the path and, mounting his horse, urged it to a gallop, distancing himself from all temptation.

When Jennifer joined her hostess in her apartment later that morning, Flora was much taken aback by her look of dejection. "Have you and Edward had a misunderstanding?" she asked without hesitation.

"What makes you suppose such a thing?" replied Jenny carelessly, as she stood uncertainly on the hearth, finding it difficult to meet Flora's searching gaze.

"Because he's found it necessary to take himself off to Fly, when I know for a fact he'd intended to return to London. When I asked him why he was leaving so soon, he told me to mind my own business, which is quite unlike him. Always most polite is Edward."

"You might say we had words," said Jenny, feigning indifference. "I find him insufferable. His arrogance is beyond comprehension."

Flora would not allow that to go unchallenged, her face coloring with indignation. "You must not speak of my dear Edward so!" she cried. "He is everything one could wish for in a brother, and I will not have him maligned."

"I tell you, he is excessively unkind!" cried Jenny, equally hotly, "and now he has left and gone to Fly without so much as a word to me."

"And what words would you have him say?"

"I don't know!" cried Jenny, stamping her foot with exasperation.

"I do." An enlightened Flora smiled. "Believe me. I do."

Jennifer stared mulishly at her hostess for a moment before making good her exit and storming to her own apartment, where she closed the door firmly behind her.

A feeling almost of desertion came over the earl as he walked the lonely pathways of Fly Hall. The house and grounds had never before appeared so empty, its portals so unwelcoming. *I must rid myself of this melancholy,* he thought. *I can't allow it to overtake my life. I must stand firm in my resolve and become more reconciled to my circumstance. It does no good to torment myself with impossibilities.*

Caesar kept pace with him, occasionally pushing his nose against his hand, but as he received no acknowledgment, he merely continued to plod at his side.

As they neared the ornamental gardens, Sinclair spied Randall in the distance and raised his arm in salute. Seeing himself thus hailed, Randall came quickly toward his employer, a grin splitting his weather-beaten countenance.

"How are you liking it at Fly?" asked the earl as his steward came within earshot.

"Very well, my lord, very well indeed," replied Randall. "It's much to my liking, if I may say so. Though I must admit there appears quite a lot of work that has been left undone in your absence, sir."

"Then I shall rely on you to set it to rights. You need not fear expense. Whatever needs to be done, see to it. Take on any staff you feel necessary, and I will expect a regular report of your progress."

"If you have a moment now, my lord, there are some immediate issues I would raise with you."

"Then we will go to my office," replied Sinclair, "and arrangements can be made."

Thus became the trend as the earl immersed himself in matters of the estate. Having no desire for the present to return to London, he found some diversion for his thoughts, and that generated a sense of purpose.

The London season was nearing its end, devoid of the presence of both the Earl of Sinclair and Lady Jennifer, and the tabbies ceased to comment on their continued absence, more noteworthy gossip replacing it within their ranks.

Chapter Nine

Returning to Fly one afternoon from a visit to one of his farms, Sinclair was surprised to see Croft hurrying down the laurel walk to meet him, his gnarled countenance wreathed in smiles, his breath coming in gasps.

Smiling, the earl waited for the retainer's panting to subside, saying, "Whatever it is, there's no need to hurry."

"There's a young lady to see you, sir," said Croft, eventually calming enough to be audible. "Would not give her name but said you would see her."

Quickening his step, Sinclair hastened toward the house. He knew not who his caller might be. There were so few ladies of his acquaintance who would call at Fly Hall unannounced, and he had to admit to a deal of curiosity.

Entering the hall, he asked of his visitor's whereabouts from an attending footman and, upon being informed that madam was installed in the drawing room, crossed the hall with a hasty step and flung wide the door. Its occupant—a small, vivacious brunet dressed in widow's weeds—came quickly to her feet, issuing a cry of delight.

"My dear Estelle!" he exclaimed with great surprise, smiling broadly and quickly crossing the room with hand outstretched.

But she ignored that hand and instead cast herself upon his breast. "I despaired of ever seeing you again, Edward," she cried, smiling up at him. "It seems so long since you left the convent to return to England."

"It does indeed seem an eternity since my return," he agreed, leading her to the chaise and seating her at his side.

She took his hand in a warm clasp and examined his features, saying, "I must admit, you look prodigiously well. When last I saw you, you were so weak that I worried continually about you, but I see now there was no need."

"None at all. Behold, I am a new man," he replied, holding wide his arm. "But tell me, how fare you? When did you return to England? Do you intend to stay?"

"I will answer one question at a time." She chuckled. "I do extremely well. I've been returned to England but a week; and, yes, I do believe I will stay."

"Then you will bear company with me," he answered enthusiastically. "I'm sorely in need of counsel other than my own."

"I had hoped to see you married by this time."

"As you see, I am not," he answered curly, not wishing to expand on the subject. Then, in an attempt to divert the conversation, he asked, "Do you open up the house in Edgemont Square, or are you retiring to the country?"

"I'm afraid both houses are to be sold, and I must look for a property to lease," she said quietly. "Dear James left me ill provided for, and so many debts have accrued while we were in Spain that I am left with no alternative. I believe myself to be almost penniless."

"His family hasn't offered you aid?" he asked incredulously. "I can't believe they would see you out of a home."

"You know they never approved of our marriage, Edward, and when I wrote from the convent in Portugal to inform them of James' death, I heard very little from them. There were no offers of assistance. They didn't even want to know the details of his demise. Indeed, the presumption is that our association is now at an end."

Sinclair issued a sound of disgust. "Thank God James isn't aware of their treatment of you. 'Tis as well you came to me. As you know, he charged me with your protection before I left the convent, and I am completely at your disposal. Whatever arrangements need be made, you can safely leave to me. I will ensure that all debts are cleared. You will have no need to sell your properties."

"I cannot allow such generosity," she cried. "Your assistance with settling his estate is all I require."

"You must permit me to honor the promises I made to a dying friend," he replied quietly. "Indeed, I will not have it otherwise."

For a moment, with tears standing in her eyes, she studied his countenance. "Dear Edward, I should have known you would come to my aid as you have done so often in the past. What would I do without you?" And, leaning forward, she gently placed a kiss on his cheek.

"What nonsense is this?" He smiled. "Whatever aid I've given to you and James is nothing compared to the support you gave to me. Without it I never would have survived." Taking her hand, he raised it to his lips.

"Now you must tell me why you've not married," said Estelle sympathetically. "I had hoped to find you most comfortably settled and on your way to setting up your nursery. If she would not have you, then she is a fool."

It took all of Jennifer's concentration to guide her horses through the ever-moving press in Regent Street. Sitting beside her, Phillip Rutledge appeared ill at ease and shuffled continuously in his seat.

"You should let me take the ribbons," he said reprovingly.

"Are you suggesting I'm not able to tool my own team?" she replied with some asperity. "For I tell you, I'm equally as capable as you."

"It's not your ability I doubt but your strength, my dear."

She cast him a disparaging look. "You need have no fears on that matter. It's by skill that I control my horses, not force. If you would but have more faith in me, you will see there is no need for your concerns."

As a landau bearing a well-known coat of arms crossed her path, she brought the equipage to an abrupt halt, almost unseating her passenger and causing him to utter a sharp oath. "What the deuce?" he snapped, frowning heavily and attempting to see the occupants of the coach that had so unexpectedly halted them, but the only view he had was of the back of their heads.

" 'Twas Edward," she replied, appearing taken aback.

"And who is his companion?" Rutledge craned his neck, but already the carriage was out of sight.

"I've no idea. She wears widow's weeds. Even so . . . she is very beautiful."

"Then you need have no further concerns for him," scoffed Rutledge. "It appears the man may all but be killed, but still he survives and obviously finds consolation elsewhere."

"Get down," ordered Jennifer. "You may return on foot. I will no longer tolerate your remarks."

"As you will, my dear," replied Rutledge mockingly. "The day has proved pleasanter than I would have supposed. Forswear, I couldn't have wished for a better outcome." Springing lightly into the road, he made a courtly bow. "Perhaps now you will come to accept the inevitable. I call for you at eight."

Setting her pair once more into motion, Jennifer left her would-be suitor to return alone. The sight of Sinclair driving with an unfamiliar female at his side had affected her more deeply than she was prepared to admit, and she mentally took herself to task. She had been returned to town but three days and during that time had continually looked for his presence. Reason told her that he was perfectly at liberty to drive—indeed, accompany—anyone he had a mind to. She had no claims upon his attentions. But that did not lessen the hurt she felt, and the thought crossed her mind, *Could this be the beauty in the portrait?*

The fleeting encounter had not gone unnoticed by the earl, and he was fully aware of who sat at Jennifer's side. However, his attention was claimed by his companion, who was constantly in need of reassurance that it was perfectly acceptable to be seen driving out while in deepest mourning.

"I would not have asked you to accompany me on a visit to the solicitors," said Estelle, full of concern, "but they confuse me, and I need a brain sharper than mine to deal with them."

"They should have waited on you in Edgemont Square," reproved the earl, "not have you driving halfway across London. They will not do so again. I will make sure of it."

"They see me as a lone female who has debts and feel that they are at liberty to treat me as they will."

"Then this will be the end of it. My man will deal with whatever arrangements are necessary in the future. You will not be called upon for a second time in this manner. I shall make certain of it. Once they see that you have support, you will not be put upon again, I assure you."

"When I am able, I will ensure you are repaid every penny, Edward. I will not have you owed such vast amounts on my behalf."

"You may have no fear," he said, patting her hand. "The amounts are not as vast as they would have you believe. I will not even notice their paying."

"But . . ." she interrupted, but he raised a finger to his lips.

"Say no more, my dear. I will not have it otherwise."

Settling back into her seat, she heaved a deep sigh. "Dear Edward, you don't know what a vast relief it is to have this burden taken from my shoulders."

Almack's Assembly Rooms in King Street, St. James', opened its doors to patrons every Wednesday evening throughout the London season. Subscribers to the exclusive club were expected to conform to its very strict rules in fear of being blackballed. Patrons were offered supper and gaming, with dancing lasting the night. However, once eleven o'clock was achieved, anyone not within its portals was doomed for disappointment, as it was then that the doors were locked and further admissions refused. Only one member of the committee acted as Patroness at any given time, the post being filled on a rota basis.

This was the penultimate event of the season, and on this particular evening Mrs. Fitzroy held the office. From her vantage point at the head of the ballroom she watched with some interest the arrival of the Earl of Hawley, his betrothed, and his reputedly wayward sister. Firm in her belief that there was no smoke without fire, she admitted to a vast degree of curiosity on the subject of Lady Jennifer's disappearance. With this firmly in mind, she decided to engage her in conversation as soon as it was practicable. She would not allow her curiosity to go unsated.

The opportunity came as the party made their way into supper during an interval in the dancing. Making her way purposefully through the press of the supper room, she approached Jennifer when she sat alone at the table.

"My dear Lady Jennifer, you must allow me to tell you how delighted I am that you are returned safely from your journey," she said, smiling and taking the seat at her side.

Feigning surprise, Jenny raised her eyebrows, replying, "What journey is this? I but visited Lady Flora Carlton and her family in Essex. It was not, after all, such a hazardous venture."

"Ah, yes, I forget, that is the *explanation* Hawley gave for your absence. Though, to be honest, I thought it had more interesting origins."

"Then I'm sorry to disappoint you, madam. His explanation was quite correct. It was no more 'interesting' than a visit to a friend."

Jennifer would have risen, but Mrs. Fitzroy laid a detaining hand on her arm and, as if noticing it for the first time, exclaimed, "Why, your hair, my dear—what new style is this?

The fashion is for short, but this is positively . . . well . . . one could almost say . . . boyish."

Before Jennifer could give an answer, a well-known voice issued from behind her.

"My dear Mrs. Fitzroy, you must allow me to comment on the subject," said Sinclair, smiling and coming to stand immediately behind Jennifer's chair. She turned quickly to look up at him, but, completely ignoring her look, he continued. "It is the new Grecian style being worn by all the ladies of fashion on the Continent, as my sister would eagerly attest. If I may offer my opinion as a mere male, I find it a most charming creation, do not you?"

Mrs. Fitzroy rose from her seat, feeling unequal to such opposition, and her smile wavered as she said, "My Lord, I was not aware that you graced us with your presence this evening. You are so rarely seen within these portals."

"I arrived just as the door was about to be locked," Sinclair informed her. "I gained admission by a mere five minutes. Come now, give us the benefit of your impeccable judgment, which I know is always to be relied upon!"

"Then I must agree with you, my lord—it is indeed a most modish creation. One that will undoubtedly take society by storm." Then, turning to Jennifer, she smiled most graciously. "I wondered at first at your daring, my dear, but now I see it at close quarters, there is no doubt it will become the rage in fashionable circles. Indeed, if I were but ten years younger, I would be sorely tempted to emulate the style myself."

"It would suit you most admirably." The earl smiled, bowing briefly. Taking Jennifer's elbow in a firm grip, he raised her from her chair. "I'm sure you will excuse us, Mrs. Fitzroy. My sister has charged me with the task of taking Lady Jennifer to her in the ballroom, and if I fail, she will be most displeased. Flora is not one to be kept waiting."

"Dear Lady Carlton. How does she fare?" asked Mrs. Fitzroy, also rising and preparing to leave.

"Extremely well, and she promises herself the pleasure of calling on you in the not too distant future, I believe."

"Then I shall live in anticipation of her visit," replied Mrs. Fitzroy with a slight inclination of her head before smiling briefly and turning to make her way toward the ballroom.

"What a complete hand you are at bamming, Ned." Jennifer chuckled, resuming her seat. "I wouldn't have suspected you to be so adept at such creativity."

"If I am, then you must lay its origins at your own door," replied the earl, an irrepressible gleam in his eye. "It is perhaps our close association over the past few weeks and your own talent for improvisation that have been my inspiration. You, my girl, are incorrigible."

"Wretch!" she cried, laughter lighting her eyes. "You need no tutoring from me. You are a complete hand at it, and I will not take the blame."

"Then shall we both confess to having a fertile imagination, Jen?"

"Most certainly, sir, but such confessions can only serve to apportion blame."

"Touché, my dear," he replied, laughing outright. "But now you must allow me to take you to Flora. She is indeed waiting in the ballroom and is all eagerness to see you."

The discord of their last meeting seemed to have disappeared, both parties preferring to forget its existence, neither having the desire to call to mind their brief encounter but two days earlier in Regent Street. Laying her hand on the earl's arm, Jennifer allowed him to take her in search of Flora. However, once the earl had placed Jennifer at his sister's side and retreated toward the card room, Jennifer felt compelled to mention the encounter to Flora.

"Lady Estelle Stratton is indeed very beautiful," agreed Flora. "I don't know the whole of it, for, as you know, Edward is reluctant to talk about his time in the campaigns, and I would not wish to press him. However, this much I have gleaned from talking to Estelle. You must know that she was extremely devoted to her dear late husband and still is. He, too, was one of Marchant's officers, and he also was wounded at Salamanca, but, unlike Edward, he did not survive his injuries."

Jenny uttered a sound of sympathy, but Flora continued. "Estelle had traveled in the column with the other officers' wives and therefore was able to be with him until the end. As you know, Edward lay in the convent for quite some while before he returned to England, and during that time a close bond was forged among the three of them. It was known that Lord Stratton would not survive his injuries, and Edward vowed his support when the inevitable should occur. When he returned home, it was with the certain knowledge that his friend would not survive above a few weeks. However, Stratton clung to life until but a month ago."

"'Tis a very sad tale indeed," said Jenny quietly, "and one can understand Lady Stratton's need for support."

"Edward can always be relied upon." Flora smiled. "Always knows what should be done."

"As I should know," replied Jennifer, studying her hands as they rested in her lap.

Flora reached over and patted them. "There's no need to be downcast, my dear," she assured her. "There is no attachment there, merely fondness for a friend."

"I'm sure that whatever their relationship is, 'tis no concern of mine," retorted Jenny, her cheeks coloring and her tone somewhat sharper than she intended.

Lady Flora smiled to herself at this show of pique and prudently changed the subject to that of a more general run of things.

Wishing not to draw attention to their acquaintance, the earl did not return to stand at Jenny's side until the evening's entertainment was nearing its conclusion. "Do you think we might venture the next dance?" he asked soberly, extending his hand and raising her from her chair.

The earl appeared unusually quiet as they waited for the sets to form. "Rutledge does not accompany you this evening?" he eventually queried.

Jennifer looked at him sharply. "Why should he? I need not be forever in his pocket."

"That's not what Hawley tells me," replied Sinclair. "I've just been speaking with him, and he informs me that Rutledge has asked for and been granted permission to pay his addresses to you."

"That is news to me," stated Jenny incredulously. "Since Ravensby, he has not approached me on the subject."

"And when he does?"

"Only then will I feel the need to consider it," she replied, annoyance rising at his words.

The music began, and they were forced apart by the movement of the dance, finding it impossible to continue the conversation until the orchestra ceased and they left the floor. By this time a feeling of indignation had arisen in Jennifer's breast, and she felt not inclined to continue the conversation, reasoning that whatever she chose to do with her future was no concern of Sinclair's. He had other objectives to consider.

As he handed her to her seat, he bowed stiffly, his countenance remaining impassive, saying, "I offer my felicitations and wish you well, Jenny—whatever course you choose to take."

"And I you," she replied with equal indifference, drawing her hand disdainfully from his clasp.

He bowed once more. Then, turning on his heel, he was gone.

Flora, witnessing the whole, heaved a sigh of frustration and was heard to mutter something unintelligible beneath her breath, but her meaning was obvious.

Defiantly, Jennifer turned away saying, "I must go in search of Arthur. Surely it is time to leave."

"Forswear, 'tis the talk of society," Rutledge informed Jennifer as they walked in Kensington Gardens a few days later. "It appears that the 'unfortunate' widow most certainly enjoys Sinclair's protection. He's forever dancing attention on her, and if Danson is to be believed, he pays her debts. *Now* tell me their association is above suspicion!"

"I will not qualify your remarks with an answer," replied Jennifer, quickening her step. "You obviously know so little of the situation that you rely on the scandalmongers for information. It's not at all what you think!"

"Are you so sure of that, my dear?" He sneered. "It does not take a great brain to see what my lord is at. Lady Stratton must be at her most vulnerable at the moment, and he turns it to his benefit. She is, as you have already observed, extremely beautiful. Sinclair would be a fool not to take advantage of the situation."

"Then a fool he undoubtedly is, for I don't believe him capable of such cavalier intentions."

"Why, 'tis you who are the fool, my dear Jenny," he scoffed. "Sinclair's no saint. He would act as any other man in the situation."

Jennifer halted and stood before him, studying his face with a slight frown clouding her brow. "Over the past few weeks I have oft thought how stupid you can be, Phillip," she said thoughtfully, "but never so much as now. You should not use your own moral code as a yardstick against which to judge others' principles."

Rutledge's countenance darkened with anger. Bowing briefly and uttering no word of farewell, he strode away, leaving Jennifer to watch his disappearing figure with some feeling of satisfaction.

Aware that she must now make her way home alone, she struck out determinedly, acknowledging acquaintances as she went but never stopping, realizing it must appear strange that she should be unaccompanied. Once having left the confines of the gardens, however, she found that her feet took her in the opposite direction than one would have supposed if she had desired to return to her home, and after a short while she found herself entering Edgemont Square.

It was a pleasant part of town, the houses offering gracious living on three floors. As she crossed the square, she was obliged to hold back to allow a horse and rider to pass, and it was with some astonishment that she recognized Sinclair. He, however, was oblivious to her presence and instead rode to a house at the far side of the square. Dismounting, he gave his horse into the care of a young boy and, tossing him a coin, instructed him to await his return.

She watched, fascinated, as he mounted the steps to the house, seeing the door opened as if his arrival had been anticipated. He entered unchallenged, as though he was a familiar visitor—indeed, one who had the right to be there.

Even after he'd disappeared inside and the door had been closed against curious eyes, she stood as if mesmerized, as if the power of movement had been denied her. Thoughts came, which she hastily put aside. Memories of Rutledge's words rose to torment her, and she leaned against the boundary wall of an adjoining property for support.

She wasn't sure how long she stood there, but eventually the earl emerged once more from the house, and she was aware that a shadowy figure stood at one of the windows, fluttering a hand in farewell. Bowing briefly in reply, Sinclair retrieved his horse from the boy and, mounting, rode in the opposite direction.

His leaving acted as a release, and she moved away, forsaking the square and making her way homeward.

"Pray tell me, dear sister, just how many suitors do you think you will find it necessary to reject before you finally decide to marry?" snapped Hawley to Jennifer over supper that evening. "Rutledge has stated his intention of returning to Buxton on the morrow if he does not hear anything to the contrary from me this evening."

She regarded him mulishly and replied, "He may return to Buxton or anywhere else he has a mind to."

"I thought you had a fondness for him. Why now this indifference?"

"Any fondness I ever had for him was purely as a friend and was soon put to flight when we became reacquainted. He's not at all the man I remember from our earlier years. Indeed, he has changed beyond recognition."

"'Tis you who have changed, Jennifer, ever since this damned betrothal to Sinclair, and even that you saw fit to end. I am completely at a loss as to know what ails you."

"Nothing ails me, Arthur. I just have no desire to be married."

"You would remain a spinster?" he asked incredulously.

"Most certainly. If it's your fear that I will prevent your marriage, then Freddie and I will set up our own establishment. We will deal perfectly well together."

"Think of what society would say," scoffed Hawley.

"Then I will inform them that I was not welcome in my own home and found it necessary to leave."

"You wouldn't dare!"

"I most certainly would; though why I should have such a desire to remain here when you make my situation untenable, I know not. Perhaps I would fare much better on my own."

"Must we continually wrangle over the situation?" he replied, throwing his napkin onto the table. "I am thoroughly out of patience with you. Once you are of age, you may set up an establishment with Freddie. I will not stand in your way. Until then, however, you will live by my dictates."

"Which are?"

"I am well aware I can't force you into marriage, but I do believe I am within my rights to most forcefully recommend that you consider it."

"And the alternative is . . . ?"

"Enough!" he cried, rising. "I will not have you dictate to me in this fashion, but beware my antipathy. You will not always find me so generous. You will not think yourself so fortunate when I find it necessary to shorten your purse strings. Remember, I have their control until you are one and twenty."

"That, for your control," she said, snapping her fingers. "I remain 'under your control' for less than fifteen months."

"No matter for what length of time, it will seem an eternity, my dear," he scoffed, leaving the room.

Sitting alone at the dining table, Jennifer's thoughts, as they had so many times since her return earlier in the day, turned once more to her visit to Edgemont Square. Sinclair had appeared so much at ease when he visited the house and, from his reception, appeared a regular visitor. She attempted to analyze her feelings, should he form a lasting attachment to the owner of the house, but the thought was too painful to contemplate. She realized now that, although she was not prepared to admit it, her affections had been engaged upon Sinclair's return from Spain, and she called to mind with great fondness their journey to Derbyshire. She dwelt on their conversations and the little attentions he had bestowed upon her. She felt a sense of security in his presence and knew she could never feel as comfortable with anyone else.

She sat thus employed until a butler gave a gentle cough behind her chair to remind her of his presence and the necessity to clear the table after the evening meal. Rising, she cast him a small, apologetic smile and retired to her apartment, not to seek repose, but to sit dejectedly in her sitting room while the embers died in the hearth.

If she could have, she would have retracted her refusal of Sinclair's offer, but it had not been possible. Since the existence of a portrait, which he continually carried with him, had become known, she feared the offer would never be repeated. Indeed, with the appearance of Lady Stratton, all hopes had died. But the calling to mind of what might have been still proved too painful to bear.

Chapter Ten

"I swear there are signs of a match there," declared Mrs. Fitzroy, when Flora paid her promised visit a few days later. "At first I thought he still held hopes of Jennifer, but I appear quite wrong."

"There are no signs whatsoever of a match," scoffed Flora. "Indeed, Lady Stratton is still in mourning, so it is unkind of you to even suggest such a thing."

"Ah, but she will not be in mourning forever, my dear, and it's seen that he wastes no opportunity to accompany her. It's rumored that he settles her debts. Now tell me, why should he, if he holds no hopes of marriage?"

"It was a promise he made to her late husband when it was known that the poor man would not survive. There had evolved a great friendship between them during Wellington's campaigns, and Edward feels it to be his responsibility that she is well cared for. He could do naught else in the situation."

"You may say what you like, my dear, but I vow, there still appears something between them. One has only to see them together."

"Then I swear you know not what you see," snapped Flora, her patience sorely tried. "My dear Edward has more sensibility than to press his suit at such a time. Indeed, I believe his affections to be engaged elsewhere."

"You don't mean . . . ?"

"You may put what interpretation you wish on my words, for I know that you will, no matter what I say, but I deem he deserves whatever happiness he can grasp."

"But of course, my dear," replied Mrs. Fitzroy enthusiastically. "I agree wholeheartedly with you. Nothing would please me more than to see him happily settled."

The object of their conversation was at that moment taking afternoon tea with Estelle in Edgemont Square after a fraught day dealing with his man of business, who had just left.

"I believe today's dealings bring to a close all claims on James' estate," said the earl. "There remains but matters of little consequence to bring about a full conclusion of his affairs. You should now be able to return to some form of normality."

"I'm relieved to hear you say so," said Estelle earnestly. "I can't continue to trespass on your good nature, Edward. No matter what promises were extracted, you have your own life to lead, and I cannot become your pensioner. I must find some way of generating an income and supporting myself."

"And exactly what do you propose, my dear?" replied the earl, laying aside his cup and sitting forward in his seat. "Just how do you envisage bringing about this income, for I assure you, it's not at all necessary. If you would prefer, I will settle an amount upon which you may draw whenever necessary, and when that expires, you need only apply for more. If you find it distasteful to deal with me directly, you may make your application through my solicitor. Would that suit you better?"

She came quickly to her feet. "Now I've offended you," she cried, contrition sounding in her voice. "My dear Edward, it was not my intention—truly it was not."

He, too, rose and, crossing the distance between them, laid a comforting arm about her shoulders. "It has been a difficult day, my dear," he said quietly. "I welcome your dependency. It allows me to repay the many kindnesses you've done me. Indeed, whatever service I've rendered is no more than my conscience would allow, and it's my most fervent wish that you become reconciled to it. How else am I to prove my gratitude?"

At that moment they became aware of a commotion in the hallway and turned toward the door as it was opened abruptly.

The footman announced Randall, who entered the room with quickened step, his countenance extremely solemn.

"What's to do now?" asked the earl sharply. "What's so urgent that you need seek me out?"

"'Tis a matter regarding Master Peregrine, my lord," replied Randall, halting as he became aware of Estelle. "It would perhaps be more prudent if I spoke to you alone, sir."

"He's injured?" asked Sinclair sharply.

"Not in the least sir. It's an entirely different matter."

The earl appeared relieved and sank once more into his chair and grimaced ruefully. "No matter what the young numbskull has been at now, you may speak quite freely. Nothing he does will surprise me. He seems determined to run the full gamut of foolish deeds, so speak up. I am prepared for the worst."

"He's been sent down, sir."

"Again!" groaned Sinclair. "Will the boy never learn? What fool-brained scheme has he been at now? I'll wager its naught but a prank."

Randall stood very erect before his employer. "He's accused of theft, sir, and has been sent down pending investigation, with the threat of expulsion."

"*What?*" the earl expostulated, coming erect from his seat. "There's not a more honest soul on God's earth than Perry. I swear he's no thief. What's he supposed to have stolen? Who accuses him?"

"A fellow pupil," said Randall, proceeding with caution, not wishing to enrage his employer. "The boy says Master Peregrine stole a valuable saber his father brought back from the campaigns."

"What use would Perry have for a saber?" scoffed Sinclair. "Indeed, if he's in need of such a weapon, he could willingly have mine."

"The young master is quite distraught, and Croft came to me saying I should fetch you, sir. He's at a loss as to what to do with him."

"I will come immediately. These accusations must be redressed. The boy must be at his wit's end."

Estelle came forward, clutching at the earl's sleeve. "If I may offer my support," she said quietly. "If you will allow, Edward, I will come with you."

"My carriage will collect you within the hour," said the earl, already on his way to the door.

The rain came in torrents, gushing from roof and piping alike as Perry watched from the shelter of a stall at the rear of the stable yard as the earl's chaise was drawn across the flooded cobbles of the yard to the coach house and the horses hurriedly taken to the stables. Caesar sat dolefully at his young master's side, unaware of the disquiet coursing through his breast, knowing only the need to comfort him by his presence.

Having great faith in his brother's ability to set all to rights, Perry's first instinct had been to run and lay all at Sinclair's feet. However, the thought of the disgrace he felt he'd brought to bear held him back. For the first time in his life he felt a reluctance to face Sinclair and instead drew farther into the stable and hid in the shadows.

"Where's the boy?" demanded the earl of Croft as soon as he and Estelle entered the hall.

"Master Perry went out some while since, sir," answered Croft. "If he's any sense, he's probably sheltering from the rain somewhere."

"It grows quite dark. Send someone out to search for him," ordered Sinclair. "I will not have him abroad in these conditions."

"Aye, my lord." Croft bowed, preparing to leave, but then as an afterthought added, "Is the lady to stay, sir?"

"Yes, have Rose prepare a chamber for her and serve her supper in the small salon. I will eat later, when I've spoken to Perry."

Seeing that the earl was much concerned and not wishing to intrude, Estelle made her excuses and repaired to the drawing room to await Rose's attentions. She could see that now was not the time to be raising questions and instead contented herself with the thought that her presence alone would lend Sinclair support.

The earl retreated to the library to pace its confines, pausing only to pour himself a glass of claret. Knowing only too well the vagaries of youth that could drive Perry to foolishness, he liked not the idea that he should have left the house when in a state of agitation. Putting his glass aside, he finally came to rest in the large chair behind the desk, his concern increasing with every minute of Perry's absence.

Seeing the servants come to the stables with lanterns held aloft and his name being called, Perry realized that he could remain hidden no longer. Deeming it time he faced his brother, he stepped out into the yard, claiming he'd been but sheltering from the downpour. He followed the servants with lagging steps, ignoring Caesar, who kept pace beside his young master, his eyes blinking with every drop of rain that fell on his faithful head.

"There's a letter, sir," said Perry stiffly, handing it to his brother, who remained seated at his desk.

The earl broke the seal and spread the sheet before him, drawing the lamp closer to give more light.

"What does it say?" asked Perry nervously.

"They request that I withdraw you from the college to save any unavoidable unpleasantness."

"Oh," was Perry's monosyllabic reply as he confined his gaze to the floor.

Sinclair leaned back in his chair, his eyes never leaving his brother's face. "I don't want you to say anything until I've finished speaking," he said in a level voice. "Then you must tell me the truth. I will not be angry if only you tell me the truth."

"I didn't do it, Ned," interpolated Perry hotly, taking a step forward. "I truly didn't. You must believe me."

"I never doubted you for one moment," Sinclair assured him, "but you understand that I must ask. There's also another matter. You promised me that if you got into further trouble, you would come to me first. Why didn't you? Are you frightened of me?"

"Never!" cried Perry. "It's just that . . ." And his voice faltered.

" 'Just that . . .'?" prompted the earl.

"It was the shame that I could have been thought to have acted as a thief. I couldn't bear for you, even for one moment, to think me guilty."

"You may be assured on that score. There's no need to convince me of your innocence," said the earl, rising to pour two glasses of claret and to press one into Perry's unsteady hand. "You tell me you did not take the weapon, and I believe you."

Resuming his seat, he indicated that Perry should take the chair opposite the desk. "How did they arrive at the conclusion that you were the thief?" he asked. "What caused them to lay the blame at your door?"

"I was seen outside Compton's rooms and subsequently gaining entrance, though I swear to you I had his permission. I went to collect some books. I didn't even see the saber. I only knew of its existence because Compton had been brandishing it in the library a few days earlier."

"Who was the witness? Who accuses you?"

"Compton's roommate, Jameson."

"If that be the case, why didn't he intervene and prevent the theft?"

"He knew I had Compton's permission to enter his room and left thinking no more about it."

"Were there no further investigations made into the matter?

Surely if you'd taken it on that occasion, it would have been too obvious that you were the thief when you were known to be alone in his room."

"Compton said that it had been in the room just before my visit, but when he followed closely in my wake, it was gone. What other conclusion could they draw?"

"There is more to this than meets the eye! You are sure no further inquiries were made?"

"Not to my knowledge, Ned."

"Was a search made of your room?"

"Yes."

"And nothing came to light?"

"How could it, if I were innocent? They were convinced that I had hidden it."

"And what was to be your motive for stealing it in the first place?"

"Monetary. It's well known that my pockets are to let, and the saber was of value."

"Then I will go to see the Principal myself. I will not allow you to be accused on so slender a case. Investigations will be made—you may rely upon it. You must remain here, but I will travel to Oxford tomorrow."

Perry grinned with great relief, his faith in his brother's abilities unshaken. "Knew you would know what to do. I know I should've come to you as soon as I was accused, but . . ."

"There is no need for self-recrimination. Thankfully, I was notified of the case and will now at least have some chance of putting it to rights. Now go and get some sleep. You look sorely in need of it."

"Devil a bit," agreed Perry, rising to take his leave. Then, as he gained the door, he turned and said simply, "Thank you, Ned."

Sinclair waved him away, not allowing him to see the grimness that had settled about his mouth.

The earl left for Oxford at first light, leaving Estelle at Fly, deeming it prudent that she remain with Perry and give him what support she may. The boy had assured him that he would fare well enough on his own, but the earl preferred that he have company to prevent him from dwelling on the case.

For the whole of the morning Perry played the dutiful host and showed Estelle over the estate, as he thought his brother would have wished. However, once luncheon had been served, deeming he'd discharged his duty, he hailed Caesar and, making his excuses, headed out to inspect the covers.

Left alone, Estelle wandered the corridors of the house, examining the portraits of the Thurston ancestors, each one bearing a striking resemblance to its predecessor. She stopped before the present earl's likeness, which had been captured when he first took his commission in Marchant's Cavalry. Her features softened as she examined the earnest young officer who showed such obvious pride in his regimentals. Drawing parallels with her own dear husband, she felt tears come to her eyes as she thought of the ravages the war had wrought on all their lives. During their time in the campaigns, Sinclair had become as dear as any brother to her. She felt it keenly that at times he appeared so downcast, when it had been her hope that, once he'd returned to England, he would be able to recommence his life.

So lost was she in her reverie that she failed to hear the arrival of a chaise and was brought to sudden awareness when she heard voices in the hall below, one of which she instantly recognized. Immediately she went to meet the new arrivals.

"Where is he?" demanded Flora of Croft. "Don't tell me he's off on one of his harebrained schemes. He should be confined to the house until the matter is settled."

"His Lordship is gone to Oxford, and Master Perry is out with his infernal hound," growled Croft, uncertain of whom she spoke.

"Arrange for our luggage to be taken to our rooms," ordered Flora, appearing not in the best of humors. "Lady Jennifer and Master Frederick are staying, and Carlton will be joining us as soon as he is able."

"I will go to look for Perry," said Freddie, making a hasty exit, determined to seek out his friend.

Jenny stood transfixed as she watched Estelle, with a welcoming smile on her face, descend the stairs, and she thought for a moment that she looked so comfortable there, almost as if she belonged.

"Estelle!" exclaimed Flora, going forward to embrace her as she gained the final tread. "Forswear, I never thought to see you here."

"I came to bear Edward company," said Estelle, "but now I see I need not have worried that he lacked support."

"Allow me to introduce Lady Jennifer to you." Flora smiled, drawing Jenny forward.

Smiling, Estelle made a slight curtsy. "You must forgive me, my dear," she said. "I did not immediately recognize you, as your hair is quite different."

"Why should you recognize me, when we've never met?" replied Jenny with a slight reserve. "Indeed, I wouldn't expect you to even know of my existence."

Estelle appeared taken aback by the coolness of her reception, but, seeing the difficulty of the moment, Flora took a hand in the conversation.

"We would not have known of the accusations if Freddie hadn't taken it upon himself to make us aware of the situation," she offered in explanation of their arrival. "We saw it as our duty to come immediately. We cannot leave everything resting on dear Edward's shoulders, and Perry must be in need of encouragement to revive his spirits."

"With so staunch a band of supporters, he will scarcely have need of me," replied Estelle. "Perhaps it would be prudent for me to return to London. I don't wish to appear *de trop*."

"I will not hear of it," replied Flora, linking arms with the widow and Jennifer and drawing them toward the salon. "We shall take some tea and discuss the situation. We make quite a gathering, do we not? At least Perry need not fear he's without support. Forswear, my sympathies are wholly with him, for we cannot doubt his innocence. Indeed, I will not allow his integrity to be questioned."

Throughout the remainder of the afternoon Jennifer continued her observation of Estelle. However, no matter what her thoughts might have been on the subject of Sinclair's bringing her to Fly, try as she might, she could find no fault with her. Indeed, by the time they repaired to change for supper, the three found themselves very much in accord on the situation.

Sinclair, upon his return some three days later, appeared much taken aback by the sight of both his sister and Lady Jennifer, who, having witnessed the arrival of his coach from the drawing room window, awaited him in the hall.

"Have no fear, you have not been invaded in your absence." Flora smiled, coming forward to greet him. "But I'm sure you must see that we had to come."

"I'm prodigiously glad that you did," the earl assured her, embracing her and dropping a dutiful kiss on her brow. However, it was Jennifer who held his gaze, and it was a moment before he could tear his eyes from her pale countenance.

"I take it that this is Freddie's doing." He smiled, putting Flora from him and advancing to meet Jenny with hand outstretched, taking hers in a warm clasp. "I hope you weren't badgered into coming. I know only too well how insistent these young cubs can be, and I'm sure Freddie gave you no option."

Jennifer smiled, unable to resist his obvious pleasure at seeing her. "Not at all. I would have come of my own accord had Freddie not had a desire to drive down immediately. When I spoke to Flora on the matter, she stated her intention of coming and asked if I wished to accompany her. Anyone knowing Perry must instantly doubt his guilt. My only hope is that you don't think me to intrude."

"Certainly not. I am most pleased to see you. Indeed, such support must not fail to revive the boy's spirits."

Flora stamped her foot, drawing her brother's attention back to her. "Enough of these pleasantries, Edward. You sorely try my patience. Tell us how you fared. Have you been able to right the matter?"

The earl sobered instantly. "I'm no further with the case," he confessed. "My inquiries were hindered at every turn, and I am still requested to remove Perry." Recollecting that they still stood in the hallway and that Croft remained, he said, "But we must not stand here discussing the matter. Come into the sitting room, and I will explain all."

"Has the weapon come to light as yet?" asked Jennifer once they were all seated about the hearth and Croft had brought in the tea tray.

"Thankfully, it has," replied Sinclair.

"Surely that must prove Perry's innocence," cried Flora.

"Not quite. It was retrieved from a pawnbroker." As Flora would have spoken again, the earl raised his hand. "A pawnbroker who, apparently, Perry has been in the habit of using."

"I can't believe that he's had the need to recourse to a pawnbroker for money," Flora scoffed. "Surely the allowance you make him is sufficient for all his needs."

"Then that shows just how little you know of a young gentleman's 'needs' while away from home. The man, Gerard, who owns the establishment, assures me that the name given was the Honorable Peregrine Thurston, and the description he gave to me fit Perry exactly. He said that Perry had availed himself of his services on several occasions over the past months."

"I still can't believe him capable of theft," insisted Flora.

"Nor I. There's definitely something that doesn't sit right. I attempted to speak to Compton, but he wouldn't even agree to a meeting, and I couldn't push the issue. The whole episode appears suspect, but the college authorities take his side in the matter. Further investigations must be made, but I am too well known by those involved to get to the bottom of the issue. I may not be able to further the inquiry, but I have one in mind who might."

"Then you must engage his services immediately," cried Flora.

"There's no need. He's already in my service," replied Sinclair. " 'Tis my agent, Randall, who worked as a runner for a while, and I believe he still has connections at Bow Street. Where better to look for a solution? He's eminently more qualified to deal with the investigation than I."

"Excellent!" cried Flora enthusiastically. "He must be set to the task immediately."

"My very intention," replied the earl, "but I must need speak to Perry first. By-the-by, where is he? The house seems uncommonly quiet. Even Caesar deserts us?"

"There's no mystery there." Jenny smiled. "They are gone with Freddie and Estelle to the kennels. They were determined that she should see the new arrivals, and, as she appeared not opposed to the idea, they went immediately after lunch."

"Oh, Lord. Estelle! I'd completely forgotten about her," cried Sinclair guiltily, sitting forward in his seat. "She must think me a very indifferent host. Almost as soon as we arrived, I found it necessary to desert her and haven't given her a thought since. Poor girl, she will wish she never accompanied me."

"I don't think there's any fear of that," assured Flora. "She's made herself quite at home and, despite the situation, appears to be very much enjoying her sojourn."

Smiling, the earl put aside his cup and rose. "Then I must go in search of them before the young numbskulls drive her to distraction. I must not be accused of neglecting my guests."

"I swear to you, Ned, I've never been near a pawnbroker," cried Perry, once more standing before his brother in the library.

"Never?" queried Sinclair with raised eyebrows. "Then how come he knows your name and likeness?"

Perry dropped his gaze guiltily. "Well, maybe, just once," he conceded.

"And that was when . . . ?"

"When I first went up to Oxford. I was short of cash, and Jameson said all the chaps did it. You were away, and I couldn't apply to Carlton for funds, so I pawned the telescope you gave me until the next quarter's allowance came through."

The earl laid his hand to his brow. "You don't make things easy, do you?" he groaned. "I was hoping you'd never been near the place and we could discredit Gerard's identification of you. As it is, you must speak to Randall. I've arranged for you to meet with him in the morning. You may see him alone so that whatever information you have to impart will be solely between the two of you. I shall not interfere, but you must be completely honest with him. To hold back on anything could jeopardize the outcome of the investigation."

"I understand and will do as you say," Perry assured him in little more than a whisper. "Though I must tell you, Ned, I am most deeply sorry for all the trouble I've caused you. I will find some way to repay you—truly I will."

"You will repay me by keeping your spirits up. I will not have you acting in this dejected manner when this whole matter is not your fault. When this is over, you may decide whether you remain at Oxford or not. I will not influence you either way. I believe it to be a decision you alone must make. In the meantime, I will not pressure you. We will prove your innocence even if it necessitates taking the whole matter to court."

Perry's eyes widened. "I couldn't bear it, Ned. To have it thrust so into the open would expose the whole family to ridicule. Even if I were found innocent, accusations would still be leveled."

Sinclair brought his hand down forcibly onto the desk. "I will not allow this defeatist attitude." He saw that the boy appeared near to tears and relented, rising to press Perry into the chair set at the side of the desk. "Come now," he said more quietly. "We must place our faith in Randall and his colleagues. I'm sure they will succeed. There are too many discrepancies in the case for it to be taken further. Indeed, it surprises me that it ever came thus far."

"I believe it to be Compton's father who insisted they find the culprit," said Perry, regaining some of his equanimity. "Compton himself appeared not to wish to press the case."

"It matters not who is the cause for your persecution. We will prove your innocence and then redress the issue. Go to bed now. I believe Randall will wish to travel to Oxford as soon as he's spoken to you on the morrow. Therefore, you must speak to him as early as possible."

Obediently Perry rose to leave, but the earl delayed him a moment longer. "Tell me, did you retrieve the telescope?" he asked, smiling. "Or does it still languish on the pawnbroker's shelf?"

"I redeemed it as soon as I was in funds." Perry grinned in return. "How could I not, when it was you who'd given it to me?"

Intent on joining his guests in the drawing room, Sinclair paused for a moment outside the closed door, listening to the pleasant hum of voices. However, it was one voice in particular that held his attention, and he stood listening to the tones as she joined in the conversation, a small smile touching his lips. The topic was of no consequence, the ladies discussing no more than trivialities, but still it held a fascination for him. He stood so for several minutes before Croft, entering the hall, brought him from his reverie, and, pushing open the door, he made his entrance.

Later that night, when all had retired, he sat by the window in his bedchamber dressed in his shirtsleeves, the miniature resting in his hand. He could not remember a time when the beloved face had not filled his thoughts. At times his longing appeared almost as a physical pain in his breast, but still he could not relinquish it. He gave a heavy sigh, realizing that the miniature's possession did naught but perpetuate the torment he felt. It drove him to question the nobleness of his motives at not throwing caution to the wind and declaring himself, but still he thought such avowals inappropriate. For as much as he'd regained his former strength, the devastation wrought on his frame was still too apparent.

Although he had in part become reconciled to his disfigurement, the thought of inflicting its consequences upon another, upon one he held so infinitely dear, was insupportable, and he tightened his fingers over the frame. Feeling the metal cut into his flesh, he welcomed the pain as a diversion from his no less painful thoughts.

He knew not how long he sat thus, or what the hour, but a deep exhaustion overcame him, and, resting his head against the winged back of the chair, he fell into a restless sleep, the portrait slipping from his fingers to lie face upward on the floor.

Coming to sudden consciousness, Jennifer immediately recognized the cause of her awakening. Hearing the earl's voice in the throes of his night terrors, she threw on her robe and hastened along the corridor to his bedchamber.

Reaching the door, she did not hesitate to push it open, but the scene before her halted her advance. Sinclair was not alone. Unaware that she was observed, Estelle bent solicitously over him as he slept in the chair and, as Jenny watched, stooped to retrieve something from the carpet and place it on a nearby dresser.

Her worst fears confirmed, with sinking heart Jennifer turned away. She would not intrude when it was so obvious she was not needed. Hearing someone running down the landing, she turned to see Perry dressed only in his nightshirt coming down its length. As he gained her side, he would have pushed her into the room before him, but she held back. He tried once more to urge her to enter, but she said with a catch in her voice, "There's no need for me, Perry. Estelle attends him." And, turning quickly, she was gone.

Confounded by her departure, Perry watched her retreat for but a moment before hastening inside. To his vast relief, he found that his brother was calming, and at his arrival Estelle relinquished the earl into his care. Assured that the terror was all but passed, she returned to her own bedchamber, leaving him in sole charge. Perry helped Sinclair to undress before finally assisting him abed, waiting only until he finally succumbed to the exhaustion that inevitably followed the terrors and slept.

As the earl's breathing became more even, Perry took his candle and made toward the door, but as he passed the dresser, a metallic glint caught his eye, and he took the object up. At the sight of it, he gave a low whistle. "So, that's the way the wind blows," he whispered to himself. "I would never have suspected it." And he returned the frame to its resting place before once more retreating to his own chamber.

Chapter Eleven

Randall left for Oxford immediately after his interview with Perry was concluded. He made no promises but assured the boy that he would gather what information he could and report his findings as soon as he was able. Perry held out no great hopes of an early conclusion, but his mind felt a little more at ease with Randall's assurance that he would leave no stone unturned in his investigations.

Sinclair took a turn about the gardens with Flora while his brother and guests entered into a game of croquet on one of the well-manicured lawns. As he moderated his pace to fit hers, she linked her arm in his, squeezing it gently to gain his attention, as his gaze was wont to wander to the players.

"You know I have a great fondness for you, Edward," she began as he turned to face her. "As a brother you are most amiable, but I must tell you, you are a fool."

"Now what have I done to incur your displeasure?" He laughed, leading her to an ivy-covered bower and seating her at his side. "I thought I was overdue for one of your lectures—therefore, speak. I am all attention."

"I know your secret," she chided, "so don't think you hide it from me. I've seen the looks you cast in Jenny's direction when you think yourself unobserved. That being the case, I would ask, don't you think you take this championing of Estelle too far?"

"I don't know what you mean," he replied defensively, declining to meet her gaze.

"I'm quite sure that you do. Surely you realize the dangers of taking all upon yourself and how it must appear to others. Indeed, to one person in particular. I would accuse you of indifference if I didn't know the contrary."

"You don't know what you know," he responded roundly. "I owe a debt of gratitude to Estelle. One that I can never repay. I'm not responsible for what others might read into my actions."

"You care not how it must seem to Jenny?"

He looked sharply at her. "Has Jenny said anything to you?"

"No, but the child would have to be a complete idiot not to have noticed the particular attention you pay to Estelle."

"Then it is all in your imagination," he scoffed. "I know Jenny well enough to know that she can be quite forthright when the occasion arises, and I believe she would have broached the subject with you before now."

"One only has to see the hurt in her eyes," persisted Flora.

"I see no hurt," he replied defiantly. "Why should she show hurt when she has Rutledge in her toils?"

"Then you *don't* know!" she cried triumphantly. "I thought you must not; otherwise, why keep up this pretext of indifference? She sent Phillip Rutledge packing. He's returned to Buxton. Now what do you say to that? Do I still not know what I am at?"

For a moment he said nothing, but then, after what appeared a moment of thought, he murmured, "Gone to Buxton, has he? There are no signs of a betrothal? Hawley assured me it was all but settled."

"None whatsoever, and if Freddie's to be believed, which I do believe he is, she would be quite happy if she never set eyes on the man again."

The earl rose from his seat, his face impassive, and said in a noncommittal tone, "Come, Flora, we've our circuit to complete before we return to the others."

Flora rose and stamped her foot with frustration. "I don't see why you treat me so shabbily and act in this sly fashion," she cried, nonetheless taking his arm and falling into step beside him. "Why won't you admit your affection for Jennifer?"

"Because, my dear, there is nothing to admit," he replied with infuriating aplomb.

For as much as he had appeared to take no notice of their afternoon's conversation, over supper that evening Flora was aware that Sinclair studied Jennifer whenever he thought himself unnoticed. However, Jenny was oblivious to his scrutiny and listened intently to some story of Freddie and Perry's telling, smiling frequently at their humor. Thus, the earl was allowed his study unhindered.

Seeing the situation, when they all retired to the drawing room after supper, Flora attempted to engineer a situation where the two would be afforded private speech. However, all her efforts were frustrated by the arrival of Carlton, who made his entrance into the drawing room issuing profound apologies for the lateness of his arrival.

"I would have come earlier," he explained amid Flora's orders that a meal should be prepared for him, "but matters of business held me in Devon."

Rising, Sinclair poured him a glass of burgundy and pressed it into his hand. "There was no need for you to travel hotfoot," he said, smiling. "However, once you are refreshed, I will explain all to you."

The hour was late when Carlton finally quit the library where he'd been in discussion with the earl. Sinclair remained alone, and, taking his glass, he went to sit by the hearth, deep in thought. He wouldn't acknowledge the sense of elation he'd experienced when told of Jennifer's repudiation of Rutledge. Even to himself, he found it difficult to admit the great sense of relief Flora's words had evoked. Possibilities that had been so long held in check flooded his mind, tormenting him anew.

He dared not believe in Flora's assumption that Jenny held any affection for him other than that of a friend. He'd fought so hard to maintain his resolve that to give rein to such thoughts brought him dangerously near casting resolution to the winds. He'd loved her too long and too well not to be tempted by the thought that his regard could be returned, but still he found it difficult to reconcile himself to the rightness of attempting to unite her life with his.

Eventually the chiming of a distant clock prompted him to put aside his glass, and, forsaking his reverie, he also prepared to retire.

Collecting the oil lamp left for his use on a table at the base of the stairs, he made his way to the first-story landing and thence along the corridor toward his bedchamber. However, the sight of a light beneath Jennifer's door brought him to a halt, and he stood for several seconds fighting the impulse to knock. Suddenly, as he would have moved away, the door came wide, and Jennifer, in a satin wrap, stood before him.

"What, you could not sleep, Jen?" he asked, an unfathomable smile twisting his lips.

"It would appear no more could you," she replied, coloring at the warmth in his tone. "I thought I heard your tread on the landing. I'd assumed you to have retired some while since but was concerned that one of your terrors might come upon you again."

His eyebrows snapped together in a frown. "Did I disturb you last night?" he asked, contrition heavy in his voice. "If so, I most humbly apologize. Although they are far less frequent, I know not when I will rid myself of these nightmares."

"I came to your door, but Estelle was before me and appeared to cope quite well without my assistance. Then Perry came, and I could see you would be outnumbered and would have no need of me."

It seemed he would have given a reply but held back and instead offered in explanation, "Estelle was used to seeing my night terrors when we were in the convent. They came more frequently and were far more violent then, and she often came to my aid."

"I see," she replied in a small voice. "She's obviously more equal to the task than I."

"My dear girl, what nonsense is this?" he cried, for the moment forgetting to moderate his voice, then looking guiltily around and adding in a much quieter tone, "I know we would be flaunting the proprieties, Jen, and the hour is late, but there are matters we must discuss. . . ."

Suddenly a door farther down the corridor opened, and Estelle stepped out, candle held high. "Is anything amiss, Edward?" she called. "Do you have need of me?"

Issuing a sound of frustration, the earl turned from Jennifer and advanced a few steps along the landing. "No, no, all is well," he assured her in hushed tones. "I but make my way to bed, and it would appear I wake the whole house in the process."

"Then I will wish you good night," whispered Estelle in return and closed her chamber door.

The earl turned once more to speak to Jennifer, but she, too, had gone. Issuing an oath, he continued on to his own room, not at all pleased with the outcome of the event.

Entering his room, he put aside the lamp and, dismissing his valet, proceeded to prepare to retire. For once he felt not the desire to retrieve the portrait. Instead, his brain was in turmoil, reliving his brief conversation with Jennifer.

It was useless denying that her words had not affected him deeply. As in common with most men, it had not crossed his mind that his actions toward Estelle could be misconstrued, for what could be more natural than a desire to come to her aid? The thought that Jennifer would see it as anything more had not even entered his head. Realizing that his motives had been so misread, he felt a strong desire to set all to rights with her. He could not bear it that she should feel that he deserted her for Estelle. He'd not been aware that he had such power over her as to wound her by his actions. When they had spoken in the corridor, the signs of her dejection at the thought that Estelle had replaced her in his need for care had come as quite a shock to him.

Although he lay in the vast bed, sleep was the furthest thing from his mind. Indeed, he wished Flora had never spoken.

"I think it best that I return to London," Jennifer informed Flora as they traversed the formal gardens the following morning. "I would not wish it to appear that I trespass on Edward's good nature. Freddie may stay if he wishes. I believe he's good for Perry and keeps him diverted, but . . ."

"I will not allow it," cried a shocked Flora. "Whatever would Edward say?"

"I believe I would be one less problem for him. He has, after all, so many other claims upon his time."

"Which you will only increase if you leave."

"Do you think so? Do you truly think so?"

"I do, and if you were to approach him on the subject, he would say exactly the same." Flora tucked her hand into Jennifer's arm and leaned confidingly toward her as they walked. "I believe I know your reason for leaving, and it is Estelle, but you must believe me when I tell you that your leaving is totally unnecessary. Why, surely you must see that there's nothing remotely loverlike between them. One only has to observe them together to realize it."

Jennifer colored and pulled slightly away so that Flora was obliged to drop her hand. "You have it completely wrong," she cried in a scoffing manner, averting her face so that her companion would not see her confusion. "You make it appear that I am resentful of their association, when I am not. I merely state the obvious, that Edward has enough concerns at the moment without the added burden of invasion."

For a moment Flora allowed her impatience to show, but to

her relief, she saw Sinclair a short distance away, heading for the stables, and she hailed him. "Edward, do come here. I have need of your support in convincing Jenny that she should stay. 'Tis her wish to return to London, but I will not have it so. I need her to bear me company."

The earl came obediently to his sister's bidding, both ladies aware of the frown that creased his brow.

"What? You would desert us, Jen?" he asked earnestly, all but ignoring his sister's presence.

Seeing the situation, Flora, thinking it prudent, slipped away unnoticed, leaving the two to make what they would of the chance for conversation.

Sinclair reached out and took Jenny's hand. "I cannot order you to stay, but may I ask it of you?" he said quietly. "No, don't draw your hand away, Jen. This is how friends should greet each other, and you have avowed that we are friends."

"Yes, yes, we are friends," she replied, attempting to smile, but further words failed her.

"Was it our conversation of last evening that drives you away?" Sinclair asked solicitously, attempting to read her countenance. "For I swear to you, I would not wish it so. I cannot bear the thought that any words of mine should wound you."

"Then you must have no fears. What words could you say that would wound me?"

He held back, and it seemed he searched for words. Eventually he said, keeping close watch for her reaction, "Flora tells me that Rutledge has returned to Buxton."

"Yes," was her only reply.

"And you do not miss his going?"

"Not at all."

A long silence ensued, and once more it appeared that Sinclair had words that remained unsaid. He retained her hand in his firm clasp until, suddenly becoming aware of it, Jennifer pulled away.

"I will accompany you to the stables," she said, more for something to say to break the moment than any desire to continue her walk.

Turning, Sinclair offered his arm, and they started along the path. "I ride out to visit one of the farms," he said lightly, taking her lead and turning the conversation toward the noncommittal. "If you would like to accompany me, I will wait while you change so there will be no need for you to chase after me as you did at Ravensby."

"I did not chase after you!" she said emphatically.

A teasing light came into his eyes. "You admitted you sought me out. Now be honest, Jen—you did, did you not?"

"Edward Thurston . . ."

Sinclair threw back his head and laughed. "That's more like it. That's the Jen I know."

Jennifer joined in his laughter. "Yes, I'll ride out with you, Ned," she said once the laughter had died down. "It will seem quite like old times."

As she would have turned to return to Fly, he detained her. "I have a great fondness for those old times, Jenny," he said with a deal of sincerity in his voice.

"So do I," she replied before hastening away.

If it had not been for the uncertainty hovering over Perry's future, the next few days at Fly would have been idyllic, but always in the back of everyone's mind was the thought of the accusations, preventing a true enjoyment of the gathering. Carlton was often ensconced with the earl in the library, while the ladies of the party talked and walked and generally enjoyed one another's company. Perry and Freddie took the opportunity for sport and were rarely seen about the house during the day; even Caesar deserted the comforts of the hearth to bear his master company on his daily expeditions.

Perry, with the fortitude of youth, had regained some of his former spirits, Oxford and its accusations appearing a million miles away. It was then with a great jolt that he was brought back to earth when a missive arrived for the earl requesting him to accompany his brother on a visit to the Dean as soon as it was possible.

Arriving with the letter from the college was a note from

Randall. He asked that his employer speak to him before his meeting with the Dean, informing him that he was to be found residing at an inn called The Star on the north road out of Oxford. He gave no indication as to what to expect, not the merest hint of his findings, and Perry thought it boded ill for his case. Surely he would have been all eagerness to put his mind at rest, if all was well.

Sinclair took a different view of the matter and assured Perry that Randall could not commit his findings to paper lest they fall before an inappropriate source. Carlton volunteered to go with them should they have need of a third party to go between Fly and Oxford at any stage. Freddie, much to his disgust, was ordered to remain at Fly to keep the ladies company and ensure that Caesar, in his eagerness, did not attempt to follow his young master.

The chaise bowled away from Fly, Sinclair and Carlton attempting to allay Perry's fears. At the house, the ladies took up their various occupations in the small salon, but their attempts at needlepoint, sketching, and reading were soon forsaken as they sat dejectedly discussing the projected meeting, not knowing when to expect the travelers to return.

The chaise with the earl's crest upon the door halted before The Star, and Sinclair stepped down. Intent on speaking to Randall alone, he had left Perry and Carlton still at breakfast at The Badger, a large inn on the outskirts of Oxford.

He eyed the building before him, looking up at its swinging sign that held a silver star, but there was nothing starlike about the inn before him. Indeed, one could scarcely qualify it by the name of *inn*—*pothouse,* more like—he thought, bending his head to enter the long, squat building. Inside, the grimy ceiling appeared low, not much above head-height, and he wondered at Randall's motives for staying at such a place.

The landlady, a scrawny individual in a greasy smock, came forward at his entrance, wiping her hands on her equally dirty apron.

"I believe you've a man named Randall staying here?" said

the earl, noticing with some distaste the way she scrutinized his person.

"Aye, I 'ave m'lord," she replied, continuing her bold examination. "Y'll find him at his meal in the taproom." And she pointed to a door at the side of the hallway.

Sinclair entered and immediately spied Randall sitting over the remnants of his breakfast, which he quickly pushed away as he saw his employer approach and, rising, made toward him.

"I hope I don't disturb your meal," said the earl. "Though I can't help but wonder at your motives at staying at such a place as this. Did I not provide you with sufficient funds?"

"All will be explained," Randall assured him in a confiding manner. "However, I think we would be better speaking away from here. Would you be averse to taking a stroll with me, sir?"

"Not in the least," replied Sinclair, relieved to be leaving the repugnant odor that permeated the inn.

Once outside in the lane, Randall fell in beside the earl, attempting to match his stride with the length of his companion's but finding it no easy feat.

Seeing his discomfiture, Sinclair moderated his step so that his agent appeared at ease. "What is it you found so difficult to say at the inn?" he asked. "I take it from your note that you've achieved an outcome?"

"I have, my lord," Randall assured him, appearing much pleased, "and it is a most favorable one. Master Perry is quite exonerated."

The tension appeared to seep from Sinclair's frame. "I knew as much," he declared triumphantly. "Now you must explain all to me. Though I never doubted the outcome, the boy will be vastly relived to have his name cleared."

The lane led them between high hedgerows, and they appeared most secluded, the earl suggesting that they rest for a moment against a stile to make conversing easier.

"You may wonder at my sojourn at The Star," began Randall, assured of his employer's full attention, "but I assure you, sir, it was necessary, for it's within its portals that the resolution of my inquiry lies. Indeed, the information was easy enough to come by, once I became aware of the situation. As you've no doubt noticed, it's far enough away from the college to be thought not to pose a threat to the school's inhabitants. However, in this, the school authorities are sadly mistaken. Each Friday night a certain group of students leave their rooms to steal away to The Star to engage in illicit gambling. . . ."

"Perry gambles?" interrupted the earl incredulously.

"No, sir, not Master Perry, but Compton and Jameson do."

"Then what has this to do with the disappearance of the saber?"

"It's quite simple, and I will state it as baldly as I am able, sir. Compton fell heavily into debt and pawned the weapon to help pay the score. He involved Jameson in the deed when he realized the enormity of his actions and how his father would survey the saber's loss."

"What need was there to involve Perry in the plot?"

"A scapegoat needed to be found to account for its disappearance, and apparently Compton often used Perry's name to avoid detection when he placed items into hock. So who better to take the blame in the form of theft? It's not until you see the boy that you realize the description given by the pawnbroker also matches Compton exactly. Neither boy was brought before him for identification; therefore, the description and name were all they had to go on."

"Have you made the Dean aware of your findings?"

"I have, sir."

"Good. Then our meeting is assured. I would not wish further unpleasantness on Perry's behalf. The boy's suffered enough." Rising up from the stile, the earl extended his hand to Randall and smiled. "It appears I am once more indebted to you."

Randall took his hand. "There's no need for gratitude, sir. I but do my duty by you and Master Perry."

"Your duties do not include rescuing my recalcitrant brother from schoolboy scrapes."

"This was no schoolboy scrape, sir. It was a serious accusation, and one I would be loath to subject the young master to if I was able to put it to rights."

"Most admirable sentiments," approved Sinclair, laying his hand on Randall's shoulder. "I am indeed fortunate to employ such a loyal retainer."

They started back along the lane, and the earl saw that Randall was grinning.

When questioned on the source of his mirth, Randall replied, "It's just occurred to me, sir, I will now be at liberty to remove myself from The Star and its delightful landlady."

"If the thought does not find favor with you"—Sinclair chuckled—"arrangements can be made that you remain a while longer."

Randall laughed. "That will definitely not be necessary. Unless, of course, it's your wish to join me there, my lord?"

Chapter Twelve

Not wishing to leave its occupants in uncertainty, Carlton was dispatched hotfoot to Fly Hall with the news of Perry's exoneration. After conferring with the Dean, the two brothers traveled to London for a few days so that Sinclair could introduce Perry to some of the sights of the city. He also thought it time that Perry be initiated into some of the more innocent forms of entertainment available to young gentlemen on the town.

Though too young to be proposed for membership, he was made known to members of the few exclusive clubs to which the earl belonged. They visited Jackson's Boxing Salon, drank in only the most fashionable coffeehouses, and shot wafers at Manton's Shooting Gallery. Perry, who was given a lesson in the masterly art of fencing at one of the most select galleries, found he had a decided flair for the sport, and badgered his brother for membership to the hallowed school. Being granted this, his final triumph was to tool Sinclair's curricle around Hyde Park at the fashionable hour. Sitting beside him, the earl showed an obvious pride in his ability, even going so far as to promise him an equipage and team of his own once he had completed his schooling.

Carlton and his news had received a rapturous reception. Flora, finding recourse to her handkerchief, declared she knew that her beloved Perry would be vindicated. Indeed, she'd never doubted it, and she blamed not Edward for indulging the boy.

Freddie would have immediately gone to join them in London if Jenny hadn't prevented it. He declared it most shabby that he was not allowed to go. Nevertheless, he consoled himself with the thought that his friend would be returned in but three days. He'd grown tired of none but female company and declared himself as having enough of petticoats, for, as he confided to Caesar, "They do naught but chatter about the inconsequential. They have no interest in the more important things in life, whereas Perry is top-rig. He knows where you might find the best sport, or buy the best horse, or indeed anything that a chap might desire, and whatever he's not familiar with, Sinclair can always be relied upon to know." Caesar regarded him with doleful eyes, not knowing his meaning, only that he was required to bear him company in his master's absence.

"You are sure your wish is to return to Oxford?" asked the earl as he and Perry left the confines of London to return to Fly.

"I'd prefer to take a commission, sir," came the reply.

"You will not!" stormed Sinclair, causing Perry to draw back into his seat at the fury on his brother's face. "If you hold hopes that I will pay your commission, I tell you now, you may as well forget them!"

"Thought you'd say that," said Perry, heaving a heavy sigh. "That's why I've resigned myself to returning to Oxford, though I must admit, a cavalry post is what I most desire."

Sinclair appeared to hold himself in check, but the darkening of his countenance proved the ferocity of his feelings on the subject. "While you are under my guardianship, you may forget all thoughts of the military," he ground out through clenched teeth. Then, as an afterthought, he added, "And don't think yourself able to enter into the Navy either. I know you— you'll try by whatever means you may to get your own way in the matter, but I will not allow it. You must put all such thoughts out of your head. It's but a phase you go through."

"Father never stopped *you*," complained Perry hotly.

"No, he did not," replied Sinclair, "and what further proof do you require?"

They fell into silence that was broken only by the sound of the horses' hooves on the cobbled roadway, but an unease still existed between them.

After some reflection, Perry said thoughtfully, "Perhaps, then, I will try the Law."

"You may try whatever else you wish," was the earl's relieved reply. "Though there's no need for you to find employment of any kind, as you well know."

"But I want to be of worth," cried Perry earnestly. "I want to achieve something rather than waste my youth."

"Your sentiments are very commendable, but we will see what thoughts you have on the subject once you've completed your stint at Oxford and spent a season on the town. Then will be the time to evaluate your future. When you are master of Fly and all it entails, you will find more than enough to occupy your time."

"Surely Fly will go to your heir," said Perry, much perplexed.

"I have no heir, save you."

"Perhaps not at this moment, but surely you will have, given time."

"Humph!" was Sinclair's only reply.

From the window of her apartment, Jennifer watched with mixed emotions the approach of the chaise containing Sinclair and Perry. She knew that their return to Fly heralded her own return to London and Hawley, but her desire to see the earl overruled that, and she hastened to the hall below to join the others in a welcoming committee. All were gathered there with the exception of Estelle, who remained in her apartment, unaware of their arrival.

While his brother lingered a moment longer in conversation with his groom, Perry was first into the hall and couldn't keep the wide grin from his countenance when he saw everyone awaiting him.

"Knew everything would be right and tight." He grinned as they flocked around him to offer their congratulations on the outcome of the dealings. To his profound discomfiture, he found himself taken into a warm embrace by Flora, who, with tears in her eyes, declared herself most relieved to have him returned to the fold.

"I couldn't have borne it if you'd been taken into custody," she cried.

"I was never in any danger of that," he scoffed, disengaging himself from her hold. "If they had found me guilty, the most that would have happened was that I would have been expelled."

"A more stupid remark I've yet to hear you make," admonished the earl, entering the hall. "Who knows what the outcome would have been? It's as well we were able to resolve the matter before it was taken further. There was none more apprehensive of the outcome than you, so don't disparage Flora's fears."

Perry looked uncomfortable at his brother's words, but Carlton came to his rescue.

"You mustn't be too hard on the boy, Edward." He laughed. "Despite all, he remained calm and handled the whole extremely well."

"And so he should," returned Sinclair. "With such support, he couldn't fail to have confidence in his acquittal."

Carlton shook Perry's hand. "And how did you fair at Manton's?" he asked. "When last I saw you, you were about to be introduced to the gallery."

As Perry would have given an enthusiastic reply, the earl interrupted. "He did tolerably well, but 'tis not a pastime I wish to encourage. He wants to join the military, and I will not have it."

"Neither will I!" cried Flora, once more gripping her younger brother's arm. "I will not have it that you follow in Edward's footsteps."

Looking considerably discomfited, Perry assured her he'd put all thoughts of it from his mind.

Carlton took Sinclair to one side. "It doesn't necessarily follow that if the boy shoots, he will want to take up arms," he said.

"I know you are right," replied the earl, "but I'm sure you can understand my way of thinking."

"In boys of his age, it's the military this week and something totally different that takes their fancy the next," Carlton assured him. "I think you need have no fear of his taking a commission."

"I can guarantee it, as I will not supply the funds," stated the earl.

Over his brother-in-law's shoulder, the earl caught sight of Jennifer standing to one side as if awaiting his notice. She'd not come forward with the others, deeming it only right that family should be the first to greet them, but, as Sinclair turned from Carlton, she made toward him to add her congratulations to those of her fellows. However, as she would have taken his outstretched hand, a cry was uttered from the stairs, and Estelle, suddenly aware of their arrival, came running down to warmly embrace the earl. He appeared somewhat taken aback by his reception but nonetheless returned the embrace. Jenny fell back, her welcoming smile fading, her hand dropping to her side as she stood transfixed by the whole.

Suddenly realizing how it must appear, Sinclair raised his eyes to hers, and, seeing the hurt there, he gently put Estelle from him.

"It's most gratifying to be received as the conquering hero," he said, smiling flippantly, holding Jenny's gaze and attempting to lighten the moment. "It almost makes the whole worthwhile."

She turned away. "I'm sure that's not how Perry sees it," she snapped. "One would suppose he would have preferred it not to have happened in the first place."

"Steady on, Jen," interpolated Freddie hastily. "Sinclair

only makes light of it. No one is more conscious of Perry's sensibilities than he."

"You are right, of course," she said generously, coming forward and once more extending her hand to the earl. "You must forgive me, Edward. It was not a tactful remark to make."

He took her hand and pressed her fingers lightly, smiling down at her. "'Tis I who should've had more tact," he said quietly so that only she could hear.

Blushing, she pulled away. "I'm sure I don't know what you mean."

"I suspect that you do, my dear," he replied, dropping his voice even lower.

"Edward, Edward," cried Flora imperatively. "Carlton has come up with the most excellent idea that we remove to Brighton, now that the London season is closed. Indeed, he's sent his man of business to secure a property on Marine Parade. Would it not be delightful if we all could go—that is, if the Earl of Hawley will agree that Jenny and Freddie should join us, and Estelle has no objection to the move?"

A general babble of agreement ensued, only Flora noticing that neither Jennifer nor Sinclair added their tones to the general consensus that it was an excellent suggestion. Perry and Freddie went so far as to declare it a ripping idea, as it would be their first season at the resort and promised all forms of hitherto unsampled delights.

Later that evening, when challenged on her thoughts of the projected scheme, Jenny confided to Flora, as they sat slightly apart from the others in the drawing room, that she doubted Hawley would agree to their going.

"Then I shall send Carlton to visit him," Flora assured her. "He will scarcely refuse his permission when approached in person, and, when need be, Carlton can have such a persuasive air about him."

"If he can be persuaded, then I would be glad to go," replied Jenny, smiling. Then, as indifferent as she could make the question, she asked, "Do you think Edward will join us?"

"Who can tell?" replied Flora. "Though I promise to do my best to ensure that he does. He never had a great liking for Brighton and its society, but perhaps the thought of a congenial gathering may change his mind." She studied Jennifer for a moment, then, leaning confidingly close, she asked solicitously, "Has there been a falling-out? There appears a new restraint between you."

"Indeed, I don't know what you mean," cried Jennifer. "There has been no falling-out, I assure you."

"Then if it's Estelle who concerns you, you may put all thoughts of a match out of your head."

As Jenny would have given an indignant reply, there appeared to be an animated conversation taking place at the far side of the room as Estelle attempted to persuade Sinclair to join her in a duet while Carlton played the piano.

"I have no voice," complained the earl defensively.

"Nonsense. You've the most pleasing baritone when you choose. I've heard it on several occasions when we were in Spain," declared Estelle.

"They were campaign songs, hardly suitable for a drawing-room recital," replied Sinclair, nonetheless appearing pleased by the compliment.

"Then 'tis settled. I know the very piece. Do you know 'The Turtledove'?" she asked Carlton enthusiastically.

"I most certainly do," he replied, taking his seat at the piano and running his hands over the keys.

Taking hold of Sinclair's hand, Estelle pulled him from his seat to stand beside her at the instrument, holding him there as he would have pulled away. But as the melody began, he appeared to relax, and soon they were joined together in the melodious strains of the song.

Their voices appeared to match perfectly, and once the song ended, the gathering called for an encore.

None seemed aware of the effect the duet had on Jennifer. Pleading a headache, she quietly left the company, but her leaving did not go unnoticed. Seeing her departure, Sinclair had the desire to follow in her wake but, much to his frustration, was prevented from following his inclination, as everyone joined the performers around the piano to add to their tones.

The following morning, having reached a momentous decision during many wakeful hours, Sinclair rose shortly after dawn and penned a brief note to Jennifer requesting that she join him in riding out immediately after she had breakfasted. Folding the missive, he gave it to his valet with the instructions that it be handed to the lady's maid as soon as possible.

However, upon its receipt, and feeling much piqued at the mode of communication, Jennifer tore it into pieces and returned it from whence it came with the added rejoinder that if my lord wished to communicate with her, he should do so in person!

Uttering an oath and disparaging all willful females, as soon as he'd been assisted into his riding coat, Sinclair strode along the corridor. Now that his decision had been made, he was impatient to put it into action, and, oblivious to Croft's questioning gaze, he rapped none too gently on Jennifer's apartment door.

As the door was opened by an inquiring maid, he pushed past her into the sitting room, demanding to see her mistress. When informed that the lady had breakfasted but was still at her toilette, he forgot himself enough to demand that she be told to hurry herself.

There had been no need for the maid to repeat his words to her mistress, as Jenny had heard them well enough through the closed door, but she went through the motions of listening to the message. "You may tell my lord," she replied in only a slightly calmer tone than his, "that I will be with him directly and will join him at the stables."

The groom preparing the earl's horse for the projected ride confided to his companion that he'd never seen the master appear in such an agitated state. No matter what the cause, he always managed to keep his temper. Quite unlike the old master, who was likely to throw whatever came to hand at your head if his will was crossed. Indeed, the earl was acting quite out of character.

Seeing Jennifer approaching across the yard, Sinclair strode to meet her, but at the sight of her pale countenance, his mood took a complete turnabout, and he appeared contrite.

"Forgive me, Jenny, for acting so imperatively, but I wanted to speak to you alone," he said, standing before her. "The house seems overfull, and we are forever being interrupted. We never have the opportunity to be private."

"And what purpose would that serve?" asked Jennifer curtly, refusing to meet his gaze and drawing on her riding gloves. "Indeed, why should it matter when you've others who would be only too willing to be private with you?"

"My God, you're jealous!" cried Sinclair, falling back in amazement.

"Certainly not," she cried hotly. "To be jealous, one needs to be . . . And I am not. Most definitely not."

Sinclair gave a crow of delight, but as he briefly took his eyes from her, she ran across the yard and, with the aid of the groom, quickly mounted her waiting horse. Almost before the earl could realize what he was at, she'd urged the horse to a canter and headed out toward the park. As he would have taken his own mount, it sidled and fretted at the leaving of its stablemate so that he was unable to mount immediately, and Jenny was out of sight before he, too, was able to leave the confines of the yard.

Seeing her some distance ahead, Sinclair set his mount at a reckless gallop, ignoring obstacles, intent only on halting her headlong flight.

He called her name but to no avail as, becoming aware that he gained on her, she urged her mount to even greater efforts, the wind taking her breath at the speed they traveled.

Realizing that she did not know the terrain as well as he, Sinclair decided to take a chance and, leaving the pathway, headed across adjoining fields, attempting to head her off before she should reach the roadway. The maneuver paid dividends. She'd slackened her pace somewhat as she entered a heavily wooded area, but as she emerged from the trees and was about to set out at a gallop once more, she found her way barred as Sinclair sat patiently waiting across the path. She drew rein and sat defiantly before him, her face flushed with the exertion of the ride.

As he said nothing but only sat regarding her with a deal of amusement in his eyes, she demanded, "Well, Edward Thurston, what now?"

"Get down," he demanded as he himself dismounted and tethered his horse to a tree. As she sat mulishly regarding some point above his head, he repeated his command more forcibly. "Get down, or do I need fetch you myself?"

That was enough to bring her eyes to his face, but as she would have given a scathing reply, he strode over and, grasping her about the waist, scooped her from the saddle, standing her none too gently on the ground before him. He stood holding her tightly to his chest, examining her features as if he saw them for the first time; then, issuing a groan akin to a sob, he covered her lips with his own, taking her breath and making it necessary for her to lean against him.

Suddenly, as if coming to realization, she braced her hands against his chest, crying against his lips, "No, Edward, no!" Immediately he released her, but she found she needed his arm for support.

"You do not love me?" he queried softly, a strange note sounding in his voice.

"How can I, when you hold another in your heart?" she cried.

"What other?" he demanded hotly. "Who tells you lies?"

"There is no need to prevaricate, Ned. I know."

"Then you know nothing. . . ."

"I know of the portrait, the one you carry with you always."

Throwing back his head, he gave a bark of laughter. "And it's on this you base your accusations? It's on this that you accuse me?"

"It is Estelle's portrait that you carry. Don't tell me to the contrary, for I will not believe you."

"Will you not, my little love?" he replied, a gentle smile

twisting his lips, and, putting his hand into his pocket, he drew out the portrait and held it out for her inspection.

With great reluctance she took it from his hand, not daring to lower her eyes from his face for fear of whose likeness she might see.

"Look," he demanded. "Then you may tell me whom I love."

She examined the portrait, and her eyes filled with tears as her own face looked back at her from the silver frame.

"Your father gave it to me just before I was dispatched to Spain," he said softly. "He thought I should have a memento of you. Little did he know how much I would come to rely on it. How it only served to increase my love for you.

"Ah, yes." He smiled, seeing the disbelief in her eyes. "Although I'd seen you on so few occasions, even before our betrothal I loved you. When our respective sires proposed the match, I couldn't believe my good fortune."

"I never knew," she whispered.

"How could you, when we were accorded so little time to-gether? I had no opportunity to try to fix your affections. You were so young and had spent so little time in society, and when I was posted, the chance was lost."

"Dearest Ned, I had no idea. Your letters gave no indica-tion, and I was desperate for some word of affection from you, but none came."

"It was so difficult to woo you from such a distance, my love," he said, smiling, "and I couldn't tell you of the horrors of war. Your letters were the only normality in my life, and I clung to them. In their naïvete they diverted me from the vio-lence of the battlefield."

"I can't bear to think of what you endured," she cried, put-ting her arms about him and laying her head on his chest. "Why didn't you tell me when you returned?"

"How could I?" he scoffed, laying his cheek against her curls. "How could I expect you to continue with the betrothal? I wanted to be the man you knew, the one you thought I was, not the wreck I'd become."

She raised her face to receive his caress. "You are no wreck, my love," she whispered against his neck. "I didn't realize I loved you until we journeyed to Buxton together and you treated me like a scrubby schoolboy. You were overbearing, high-handed, provoking, and you broke my heart. Until then I wasn't aware of just how dearly I loved you."

"Then why did you refuse me when I offered for you?"

"I thought you only offered out of honor, that you thought you'd compromised me."

"It was no such thing." He smiled. "Though I must admit, I did it badly." Taking her hand, he raised it to his lips. "Now I will ask you that question again, Jen."

"I will consider it." She chuckled, evading his embrace. "I will give it my honest consideration and give you my answer in a few days."

"You will . . . *what?*" he cried in disbelief. "No, you won't, my girl. I will have your answer now, or you will pay the consequence. Will you have me or no?"

She looked at him mischievously, feigning deliberation. "I must first take into consideration this propensity you have for keeping portraits of unknown females. . . ."

"Jen . . ." he warned, taking a step toward her.

"Very well, dearest Ned, I will have you."

He reached out to her and snatched her to him, kissing her fiercely until they fell breathlessly apart.

"Damn it, Jen, you terrified me." He chuckled, sinking to the ground at the base of a tree, a lock of damp hair falling across his brow, which only served to make him appear all the more vulnerable. "Forswear, I've never been so frightened in all my life." He held out his arm that she would join him.

"How was I to know it was *my* portrait that you carried?" she cried, spreading wide her riding skirts to sit beside him. "Edward Thurston, I . . ."

"No, you don't, Jen. You know you don't." He laughed, pulling her roughly to him.

"Well, perhaps not, Ned," she conceded, making no attempt to withdraw from his embrace, "but at times I have so wished to box your ears."

"Then box away, my love"—he laughed—"for 'tis naught but your way of proving you love me."

"And I do, Ned, most truly I do," she vowed, winding her arms about his neck and pulling his head down to hers.

As they rode slowly homeward, it was agreed that they should keep their secret until Sinclair had spoken to Hawley.

"And then we will surprise them all, sweetheart." He smiled.

"It will come as no surprise to Flora," said Jenny. "She has guessed it all along."

"Then we will keep her guessing a while longer, for she cannot be relied upon to keep her triumph secret."

Arriving in the yard at Fly, they were met with the information that Lord Carlton had left for London.

"Damnation, I would have gone in his stead," declared Sinclair, dismounting.

"It will make no matter." Jenny smiled, doing likewise. "And I will have your company a while longer."

"Aye, tomorrow will do as well," he agreed, resisting the temptation to put his arm about her waist as they left the yard. "I will not leave my girl quite so soon."

During the evening Flora cast them several inquiring glances, but as she was met with naught but a noncommittal smile, she remained in ignorance of the true state of affairs and retired to her bed none the wiser of the events that had taken place.

Chapter Thirteen

"**C**onfound it, Sinclair, does your family intend to descend on me *en masse*?" snapped Hawley when the earl was ushered into the library. As the earl would have replied, he raised a hand. "There's no need for your pleadings; I will tell you exactly what I told your damned brother-in-law. Jennifer and Freddie do not go to Brighton. They return to London immediately. Indeed, my coach is already on its way to collect them."

"It's not on that issue that I requested this interview," replied Sinclair, keeping his calm only with great effort. "I come on an entirely different matter, though 'tis one I believe will find favor with you."

Hawley rose from his chair behind the desk to pour himself a glass of burgundy, but he made no offer of refreshment to the earl. "And what is it that you think will find favor with me?" he asked with a sneer, returning to his seat. "I am most eager to hear it."

"I will not prevaricate; Jennifer has agreed to marry me."

Hawley's face suffused with color. "You approached her without my permission? That was extremely unwise. While she's under my guardianship, there's no way on this earth that I'll agree to your marriage." And he brought his hand down forcibly onto the desk.

Bearing in mind Jennifer's words, Sinclair tried a different tack. "I would have thought it to your advantage to see her creditably settled. Will it not then leave you free to pursue your own nuptials? Indeed, Freddie may live with us at Fly; even he will not be allowed to hinder you. You will be free of all responsibility."

"You may not be aware, but my own betrothal is at an end," snapped Hawley. "Therefore I gain nothing by allowing this marriage. Indeed, I would be loath to allow my sister to ally herself with such as you. She deserves more than half a man."

Sinclair started forward, fury showing in his every line, his intent only too obvious.

Hawley sat back in his chair. "Do not think to attack me in my own home," he warned. "My servants are well within hailing distance, and nothing would please me more than to have you manhandled from my house, which I assure you I would have no hesitation in doing." Extending a hand, he rang a bell, and immediately the door was opened. "My lord is leaving," he informed the lackey. Then, turning to Sinclair, he added, "Your method of leaving is entirely in your own hands."

"The matter does not end here," the earl assured him, realizing the futility of attempting to prolong the interview. Turning on his heel, he left Hawley to contemplate the situation alone.

Which he did at great length, his own state of rejection paling into insignificance. Convinced of the humiliation he was sure the earl was presently suffering, he congratulated himself on the great piece of fortune that had laid revenge within his grasp.

However, in this particular he was quite wrong. The interview had not so much left the earl in a state of dejection but in one of extreme determination. The thought that if Hawley had already dispatched his chaise to Fly, his beloved should be returned to London before morning, did a deal to appease his mood. Hawley would not be able to keep her under lock and key. At worst, his opposition would only be allowed for the length of his guardianship, which in not much more than a twelve-month would be at its end.

Presenting himself once more at the Earl of Hawley's door the following morning, determined to see Jennifer, he was informed that the lady was indisposed and unable to receive visitors. When asked to qualify the indisposition, the servant relayed the news that he believed her ladyship was overly tired from the previous day's journey.

Assured that his intended was indeed well and that the denial was issued at Hawley's instigation, the earl removed himself to White's, determined that it should not appear to Hawley that he languished in any way.

However, this became the pattern over the next few days. Each morning he would arrive at his lordship's door, only to receive the same rejection, the excuses ranging from the lady had a headache to the lady was attended by the mantua-maker, and his patience began to wear thin. He knew not whether she was aware of his calls, but he felt some effort must be made to contact her. Perhaps Freddie could be the solution, but Freddie was nowhere to be found. He searched in all the likely places he thought the youth would frequent but drew a blank. He returned to Fly Hall both irritable and weary, having left messages about the town that Freddie should contact him on a matter of urgency.

Supper proved a solemn, solitary meal, and at its conclusion he retired to the library, ordering a decanter of brandy. He seldom drank to excess, never feeling in need of the solace of spirits, but tonight he drank steadily, his mood turning to the morose. The hour advanced past midnight, and still he remained seated on the hearth, the candles burning low in their sconces, the night air turning chill. Suddenly a discreet tap came on the door, and the footman entered to announce Master Frederick Lynton.

"At last," was Sinclair's relieved reply, not realizing the incongruity of the visit at so late an hour. However, when the figure of the youth entered, he leaped from his seat in amazement and crossed the room to gather the youth to his breast.

"Jen!" he cried. "My God, Jen." And he held her tightly to him.

"You must let me breathe, Ned," she cried between laughter and tears as she clung to him. Smiling indulgently, she pushed him toward his chair and said, "Sit down." Which he did, drawing her to sit on his lap and holding her there. She was not averse to her situation and quite happily nestled against him.

However, once the joy of reunion allowed, Sinclair gave a rueful grin. "As you may have noticed, my dear, I'm decidedly half-sprung," he confessed.

"The thought had crossed my mind," she said, chucking softly. "Why is it, Edward Thurston, that whenever I am in need of you, I find you foxed?" She shook her head slightly, a small frown puckering her brow. "No, that's not right," she said, correcting herself. "I believe the term is *bosky.*"

"The term on this occasion is *foxed,* decidedly *foxed,*" he replied, grinning unrepentantly. "Otherwise, I wouldn't be allowing you to sit unchallenged on my lap, when I should, in all propriety, return you home."

"I am not going home," she declared blithely. "I shall never go home again!"

He frowned heavily. "However much we would wish it, you cannot remain here, my love. I will not allow you to discredit yourself for my sake, for you would be quite ruined, no matter what the outcome."

"I'm not remaining here, and neither are you. We join the coach once more."

"We travel north *again*?"

"Most certainly!"

"You go to Rutledge?" he demanded, coming upright in the chair and almost unseating her from his lap.

She smiled lovingly, laying a hand against his cheek. "What a goose you can be, Ned. We go to the border."

"The border?" he queried in a befuddled manner. Then, as

understanding came, he cried with delight, "Gretna Green . . . By Gad . . . We elope!"

"The light dawns." She chuckled, unable to contain her amusement. "I will remind you of this conversation when we are quite old and staid, and you will not believe it ever took place."

"But what about Hawley?" he asked, sobering.

"*This* time I have left a note. It states that I've gone to Brighton. He will no doubt spend several days searching for me there before realizing that he has been duped, and then it will be too late. He must make what best he can of the situation."

"He's that stupid?" asked Sinclair in disbelief.

"Most certainly, he has neither an imagination nor a romantic soul."

"Which you have in abundance, sweetheart." The earl laughed and would have kissed her again, but, disengaging herself from his embrace, she stood before him, hands on hips.

"Edward Thurston, if we are to elope, I suggest you make some effort to prepare for the journey. And before you ask, yes, I do have a suitable gown."

He smiled, coming unsteadily to his feet. "You are very resourceful, my love. Your brain, at the moment, is much sharper than mine. Tell me, do we travel post?"

"Certainly not," she said, laughing as she urged him toward the door. "We travel by the Accommodation Coach. What other way does one travel to one's wedding?"

"Exactly!" he agreed. "I wouldn't have it any other way, Jeremiah!"